5 reasons you'll lo

A pacy, exciting story. Can Noah save his Wilderness?

Including some fun ideas for things to do outside from **Nature Detectives**

A heart-warming story about friendship, the importance of wild, imaginative play, and standing up for what you love

A beautiful celebration of the wild spaces around us

Julia Green evokes the natural world with her wonderfully lyrical writing style

A letter from JULIA GREEN

Wild places have a special magic. As a child, I played outside with friends and my sisters in our garden, in the fields and on the wild common a short walk from our house. We made a wonderful secret den in the woods, under an oak tree. The stories I loved were often set in wild places, too.

Now I'm grown-up (on the outside, at least!) I still love best the times I can be outside: walking along a huge empty beach by the sea, or on a cliff top, up a high hill, in fields or woodlands. Being in wild places seems to connect me with who I really am, makes me happy, calms me and helps me to see what really matters.

My story celebrates a wild place in the middle of a city, and a group of children who play there. It is inspired by a real place, and a real group of children, though I have taken many imaginative liberties with my fictional version.

When you have finished reading the story, I hope you will want to run and play outside, look at the sky, breathe in deep, build a den, climb a tree and NOTICE the beautiful, ordinary world all around us.

Julia Green

This story is dedicated to
the original children in our street
(J, J, L, S, M, M, E, A & E)

OXFORD
UNIVERSITY PRESS

Great Clarendon Street, Oxford OX2 6DP
Oxford University Press is a department of the University of Oxford.
It furthers the University's objective of excellence in research, scholarship,
and education by publishing worldwide. Oxford is a registered trade mark of
Oxford University Press in the UK and in certain other countries

First published 2016

British Library Cataloguing in Publication Data
Data available
ISBN: 978-0-19-274365-7

1 3 5 7 9 10 8 6 4 2
Printed in Great Britain
Paper used in the production of this book is a natural,
recyclable product made from wood grown in sustainable forests.
The manufacturing process conforms to the environmental
regulations of the country of origin.

THE WILDERNESS WAR

JULIA GREEN

OXFORD
UNIVERSITY PRESS

The children in the Pear Tree Buildings:

"in Wildness is the preservation of the world"

(Thoreau)

What would the world be, once bereft
Of wet and of wildness? Let them be left,
O let them be left, wildness and wet;
Long live the weeds and the wilderness yet

(Gerard Manley Hopkins, Inversnaid)

Noah's look out tree
(Hill slopes from right to left & north to south)
Bamboo
Fire
Pond
Toby's trench den
Asha & Anil's
tepee den
Boggy patch
Bramble maze
Old
Pear
Tree
Greenhouse
Holly & Nat's
pirate boat den
Pear Tree Buildings
1
2
3
4
5
6
7
8
9
10
11
12
13
Asha &
Anil's
house
Toby &
Holly's
house
Mr Moss's
house

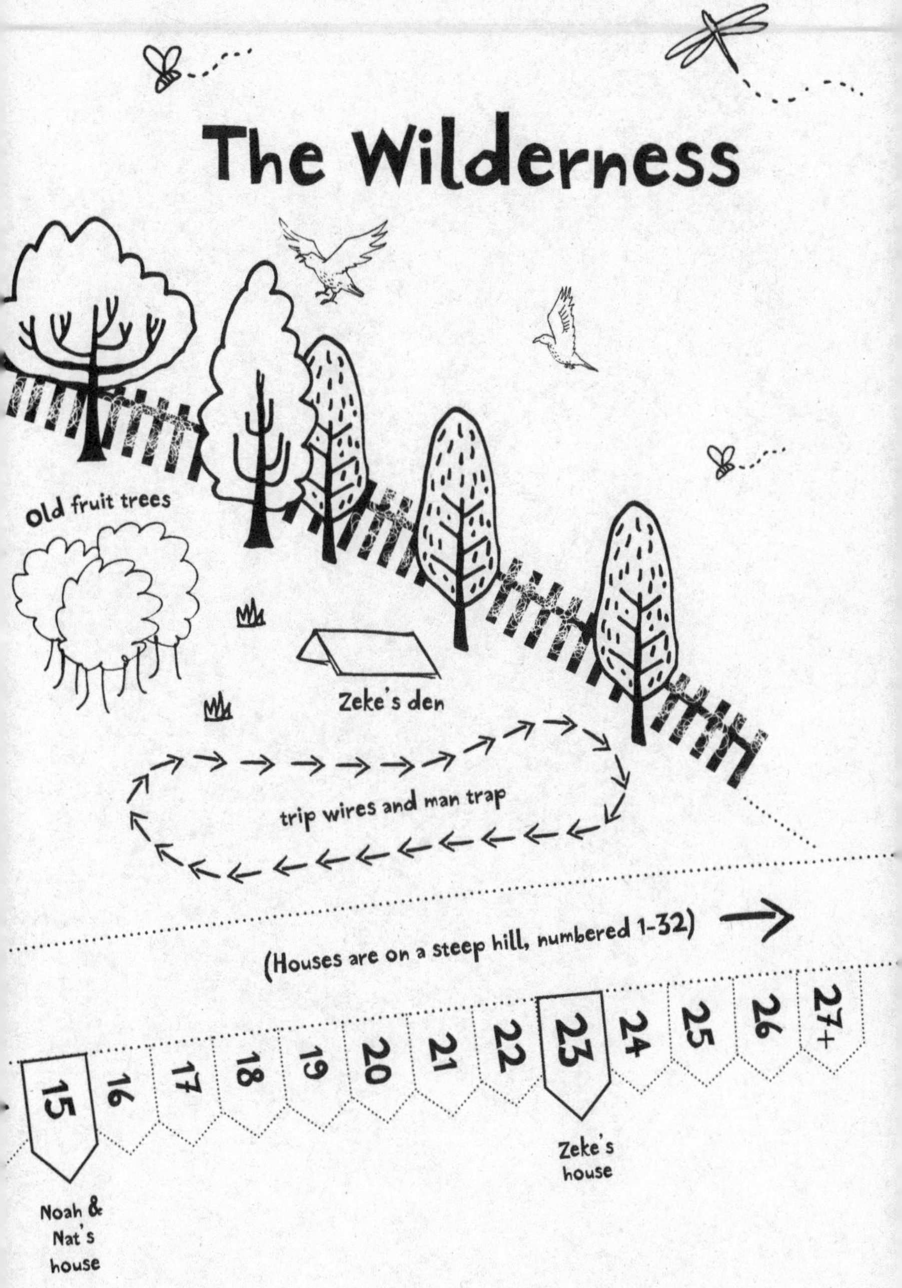

The Wilderness

Old fruit trees

Zeke's den

trip wires and man trap

(Houses are on a steep hill, numbered 1-32)

Noah & Nat's house

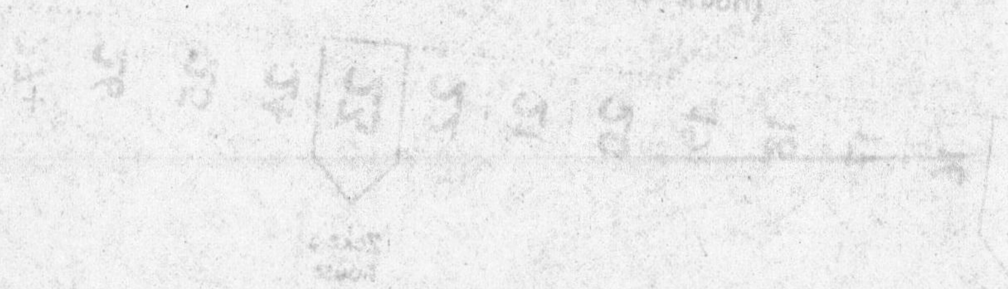

Friday 25th July

Chapter 1

Noah closed the front door behind him. He sniffed the air, the way an animal might.

Early morning. So early, the roar of traffic hadn't started up yet, and he could hear birdsong. He ran down the path onto the pavement, squeezed between the cars parked on the street and ran across to the other side.

The long grass was dripping wet from dew. Noah ducked under the low branches of the old pear tree and pushed further into the patch of rough overgrown land he called the Wilderness. His hand accidentally brushed a stinging nettle and he winced. He rubbed the place with spit to stop the itchy pain.

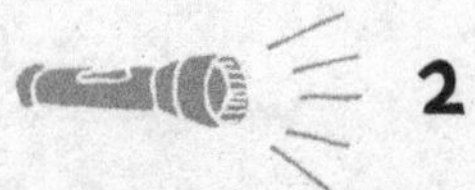

Ahead of him in the deep shadow under the trees something moved.

Noah crouched down behind the net of brambles to watch. The hair on the back of his neck bristled.

What was it?

Something bigger than a fox. Not a person.

His heart thudded. He watched, and waited.

A deer stepped out of the shadows into a pool of sunlight.

Noah blinked, to be sure it was really there.

Slanting sunlight spilled through the green canopy of trees at the bottom of the Wilderness. The deer stood completely still, a dark shape silhouetted against the light. It stared directly at Noah.

He saw the way its sides heaved slightly as it breathed in and out, as if it had been running. He saw the deep pools of its eyes, and the furry edges of its ears, and its breath rising like steam. It was a young deer: Noah could make out two small antlers, stubby growths that one day would be big and forked, like branches.

They looked at each other, deer and boy: a moment that felt like recognition, as if something had passed between them.

Noah's own breath steadied and slowed. He blinked.

And in that second, the deer had gone. Disappeared totally, as if it had dissolved into nothing in the warming air, leaving no trace.

How had it even been there in the first place?

Already, Noah began to doubt himself.

And yet it had seemed so real . . . as if he could have reached out his hand, and touched its warm fur.

Even so, he wouldn't tell the others about the deer. Not yet. Just in case it hadn't really been there at all.

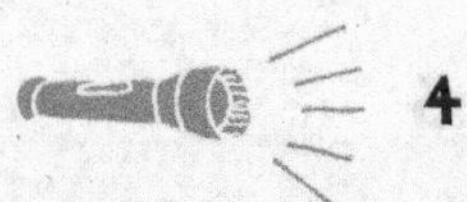

Chapter 2

Today was the last day of school before the holidays began.

Six weeks of freedom.

All day, while they tidied up the classroom, and had the end-of-term assembly, and his teacher talked about holidays and the summer reading challenge at the library, Noah thought about the deer, and the Wilderness.

Tomorrow, they would start work on their dens. Toby and he would clear the tunnels in the bramble maze. They would make fires, and camp out all night. Noah, and all the children in the street: Toby, and his sister Holly, and Zeke, and Anil and Asha, and even Noah's little sister Natalie.

Once school was over for the summer, they would play outside all day and into the night.

Excitement flared in Noah's chest. It was all about to begin.

Tonight, they'd play his favourite game of man-hunt, and stay out till long after dark.

Toby had invented the game. It needed torches and darkness, and in summer it wasn't dark enough till after nine and on normal school days none of them were allowed to stay up that late. So, the first night of the summer holidays meant the first man-hunt, too.

The idea was to get to the base (the pear tree) before anyone on the other side shone their torch to catch you, and at the same time, you had to try to catch out the other team with your own torch. It involved stealth, speed, and good powers of hiding, and knowing when to break cover. In the dark, everything became more exciting and scary. Noah could hardly wait!

*

Now, at last, it was dusk.

Noah crouched behind the bramble thicket, heart thudding, eyes straining into the half-darkness.

Someone was creeping up the hill next to the fence,

someone good at stalking which probably meant Holly or Toby. Only, Holly was on his side, so Noah had to wait to be sure; he mustn't make a mistake.

Noah rested his hand on the torch switch, ready. He had to stay hidden. He waited and listened. He was good at this. He'd practised.

An owl hooted. Or was it someone—Zeke perhaps—pretending to be an owl? Noah glanced up at the trees. They were black against the navy blue of the sky. There was a bird up there—not an owl, but a crow, balanced on the edge of the big nest in the ash tree.

A twig cracked. Noah stiffened, all senses alert.

There was a rush of movement, and voices called out.

'Got you!' Anil ran into the open, shone his torch on the figure squirming against the fence.

'Not fair!' Holly cried out.

Noah saw her face, ghostly in the torchlight.

Anil laughed and sprinted away before Noah had the chance to catch him. But already Toby was galloping down after Anil. The Wilderness flashed with light from different torches, and above all the other voices yelling and calling out, came Natalie's screams. 'Ow! Ow! Ow!'

Natalie. His little sister. Typical.

This was her first time playing out late with them all. Noah was supposed to be looking out for her. He'd promised Mum. And he'd forgotten her completely.

Holly was already with her under the pear tree, sorting her out, soothing her and finding dock leaves. Good. He didn't have to stop playing after all. Anil and Toby were out, caught by each other. So, that just left him, Asha, and Zeke.

Noah could take advantage of the kerfuffle around Nat to move his position. He shifted his feet, aware of every tiny sound. The ground was sticky, muddy: he was near the boggy patch. The entrance to the bramble den was just over there—if he crept inside, he could wriggle through the tunnel and come out higher up the hill, close to base.

Was that the sound of a frog in a puddle? Or someone throwing a stone?

A breeze rattled the bamboo stems over to his left. Noah shivered.

He heard footsteps moving over grass, stealthy and determined. His heart pattered against his ribs. This time, he was the prey. He crouched down to feel for the entrance to the bramble tunnel—too dark to see anything now. And just

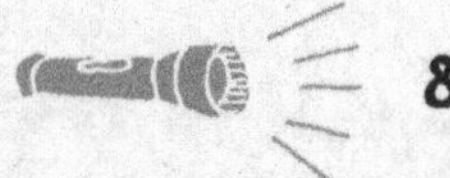

when he thought he'd found it—only so prickly and overgrown—Ouch! His foot caught in a loop of bramble, he stumbled, and the movement gave him away.

Light blinded him.

'Got you!' Zeke crowed. He ran over, thumped Noah on the back. 'Sorry, mate!' He grinned.

*

Nat was sitting under the tree with Holly. 'I got stung really badly!' she told Noah. 'Look!' She stuck out her leg to show him.

'Too dark to see,' Noah said. 'Anyway, it's only a nettle rash.'

'It still hurts a LOT, you meanie.'

'You wanted to play out with us. You'll have to toughen up, Nat.'

'One more game, everyone?' Toby's voice came from the tree, above them. He clambered down through the wizened branches and jumped the last bit. In one hand he held a newly sharpened stick. Toby never went anywhere without his penknife; whittling sticks to a sharp point was his speciality.

'New teams?' Toby hopped from one foot to another, a

kind of war dance. 'Boys versus girls this time?'

'Not fair,' Holly said. 'There's more of you. Not that we wouldn't thrash you lot.' She looked around. 'Anyway, Asha's still hiding. She's the winner. She gets to choose teams. Asha?' She called out, and the name bounced back in echo. 'ASHA! . . . Asha . . . sha . . .'

'She's gone inside, I think,' Anil said. 'I'll go and check.'

They watched him run down the hill to number five. The darkness swallowed him. 'Funny, the way he always knows about Asha,' Zeke said.

'It's a twin thing,' Holly said. 'Not only do they look the same, apart from Asha's long plait, but they are so close they know what each other thinks.'

'I wish I was a twin,' Nat said.

'I'm glad you're not.' Noah imagined two Nats. Two too many little sisters.

'Let's plan tomorrow,' Toby said. 'Who's up for working on the bramble maze? Clearing the tunnels and stuff.'

'I am,' Noah said.

'Nat and me are going to make our den, first,' Holly said. 'We can help you later.'

'It's a *ship* den!' Nat jumped up and down. 'It's going

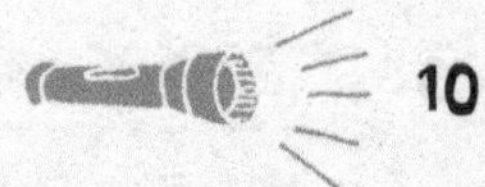

to be brilliant! I've drawn a plan. It's got sails and a mast and a treasure chest and mermaids and fairy lights and everything.'

'Cool,' Zeke said.

Noah glanced at him. Was he being sarcastic? Or just kind?

'OK Nat,' Noah said. 'You're all sorted. Good. Now shush.'

Anil emerged from the shadows. 'Yep. Asha got too cold, went in. Mum says I've got to come in now too.'

'We're planning dens and the bramble maze for tomorrow,' Holly explained.

Anil nodded. 'OK. See you then. Night, everyone.'

Nat yawned loudly.

'I'll take you to your house,' Holly said. 'Unless Noah's going in?'

'Not yet.'

Toby was already trailing down the hill, catching up Anil.

Noah watched everyone go: Toby to number seven, Zeke up to number twenty-three, Holly giving Nat a piggy-back on her way home.

Noah wasn't ready to go inside. Not this first night, the beginning of the holidays, the best night of the whole year.

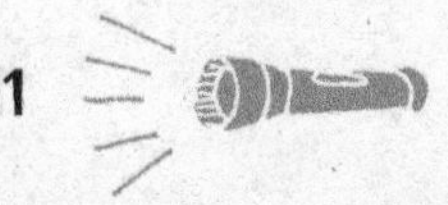

He walked slowly up the hill on the edge of the Wilderness towards the old greenhouse with the broken windows.

He pushed the door and it creaked open. He breathed in the dry papery smell of old pots and dusty wooden shelves and dry earth. He loved that smell. He stood for a moment in the doorway, staring into the darkness beyond, enjoying the silence, the sense that the whole Wilderness was his.

He remembered the deer—all day, it had kept coming back to him, making his spine tingle: the feeling of looking into the eyes of a wild creature that for one moment was not afraid of him. Would it come back tonight? Could he stay out all night, to see? Sleep here in the dry dusty greenhouse, so he'd be ready for dawn . . .

But Mum would notice. She'd be waiting for him now, expecting him any minute.

Not tonight, then.

Noah left the greenhouse behind and pushed on through the tall grass, further up the hill towards the top of the Wilderness. They didn't play up here so often: they usually stayed on the land opposite their own homes, between number twenty-three (Zeke) and number five (Anil and Asha).

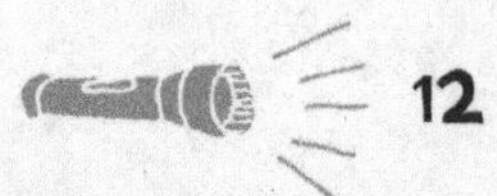

He waded through patches of tall flowering weeds called rosebay willowherb, caught his clothes on thistles he couldn't see properly in the dark.

The birds were silent, at roost. The city noises had died down too: just a few cars along the main road, and the dog barking from the flats, the drone of an aeroplane coming in to land at the airport.

Mothy things blundered about; the grasshoppers still whirred. Something clicked as it flew close to his face; Noah ducked.

A bat flitted low across the grass, catching the moths. Noah knew it was a bat not a bird, because of the jerky flight, and the thin high sound it made, too high-pitched for a grown-up's ears. Horseshoe or pipistrelle? He couldn't tell. But brilliant, to see a real live bat. He'd tell the others in the morning. Not about the deer, though. That would stay a secret for now. Just till he was sure.

Noah kept moving, almost sleep-walking now. He wondered if he'd see stars soon, and the moon rising . . . imagine this all flooded in silver . . .

His foot bumped into something hard.

He wasn't expecting that.

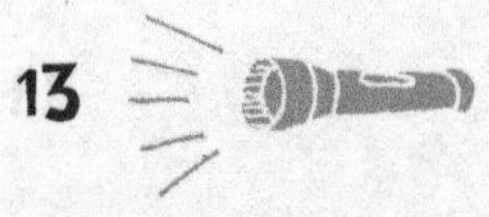

Not a tree, or a log, or a stone. It was round and smooth and solid: a post. And at the top, a card—white paper laminated in plastic, tied on with plastic ties. Writing.

Even in the dark he could make out the big letters at the top.

Fear cascaded down his spine in horrible shivers. The letters spelled out three terrible words.

LAND FOR SALE.

Chapter 3

Noah took the torch out of his pocket and shone the light on the words so he could read everything, even the small print at the bottom of the notice. It didn't make much sense at first. It was written in an old-fashioned style with long sentences and things called sub-clauses. Noah stumbled over some of the words, but gradually he worked it out.

The Wilderness was for sale, as a place to build houses.

The notice didn't call it the Wilderness. It called it 'derelict land suitable for building plot for houses.'

For a second, Noah couldn't breathe properly. The idea of someone building houses here, strangers trampling over their Wilderness and spoiling it for ever . . .

Noah raced down the hill to tell the others. But the front doors of his friends' houses were all shut, the windows dark with closed curtains and no lights showing. It was too late. Everyone had gone to bed. He'd have to wait till morning.

He ran back up to number fifteen, and threw open the door. 'Mum?'

The house was silent, dark.

He kicked off his muddy trainers and raced upstairs.

A strip of light showed under Mum and Dad's bedroom door.

'Mum?' Noah called again.

'At last, Noah!' Mum sounded cross. 'Get straight into bed. Have you any idea how late it is?'

'Sorry,' he tried to say. His voice came out croaky.

'We'll talk in the morning,' Mum said.

Noah ran along the landing, past Nat's room, and up the steep stairs to his attic. He flung himself on the bed and lay there. His chest was tight, like when you need to sob, but he wouldn't let himself. He needed to think. He needed a plan. Once he had a plan, he could get into bed properly and sleep, and in the morning he would tell everyone and

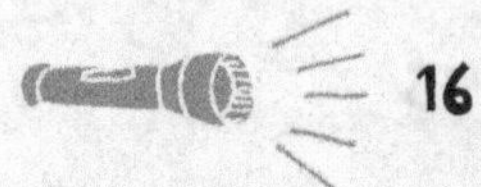

they could start doing something, together, to stop the Wilderness being sold and built on.

Cos that was what they had to do. No question. Noah had never felt so sure of anything in his whole life.

But how?

His mind whirred and churned and clunked.

Barriers? Build a high wall out of logs and branches and old doors and stuff off the dump, so no one could get in? With watch-towers, to warn of approaching danger?

Attack the builders with sharp sticks and catapults? Toby was an expert on making weapons . . .

Would that be enough?

Noah climbed across the bed and pushed opened the big skylight window in the slope of the roof. He stuck his head right out and took a deep breath of night air. Up here, he was closer to the Wilderness trees and the open sky. The wind had got up; the branches of the tall ash trees swayed and rocked the birds' nests back and forth.

Yes!

Seeing the crows' nests gave him an idea.

Tomorrow, he'd build a lookout in the tallest tree, so he could spot any enemy intruders. Everyone else's dens could

be places to hide and spy from, too. They'd spread them out all over the Wilderness, a circle of protection.

Toby and the others would have more ideas.

Noah leaned right out of the window, so he could see the whole stretch of the Wilderness. It ran the length of the street, the other side of the road, in total darkness now.

This night should be the best one of all, with six wild, wonderful weeks of freedom stretching ahead. And instead, it was as if someone had kicked him in the stomach.

But he'd fight back. They all would. There was no way they were going to let someone destroy the Wilderness and build houses on it.

He propped the window open and climbed under the duvet.

He was too hot. He peeled off his clothes and lay down again and turned the pillow over to find a cool patch. His mind was whirling again, but mixed up with dreams, now . . . the deer was there, staring at him with its dark eyes, pleading for him to do something . . . he reached out to touch its smooth furry nose but . . .

No, it was still too far away.

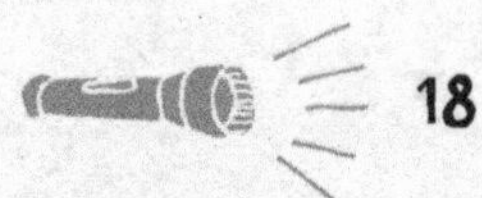

Saturday 26th July

Chapter 4

Craaw . . . Craaw. A crow landed on the rooftop, calling in its croaky voice and waking Noah. Its claws clattered on the tiles.

Noah untangled his feet from the scrunched-up duvet. He reached for his clothes from the tumbled heap on the floor. He pulled on yesterday's muddy jeans and T-shirt and whizzed down the steep attic stairs backwards, like on a ship's ladder.

The house was silent. No one was up. He could sense how early it was. If he hurried, he might see the deer. And then with a horrible lurch he remembered the For Sale notice, and a sick ache settled in the pit of his stomach.

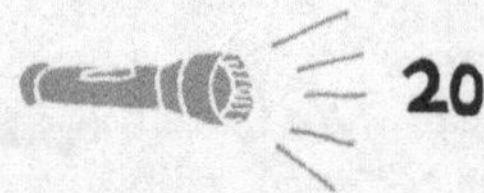

But he must check for the deer first. He'd miss his chance if he left it any later.

Noah put the front door on the latch, squeezed between the parked cars outside, ran across the street and dived deep into the Wilderness.

Behind him on the rooftop the crows screeched and chattered. Noah glanced back at them for a moment: two parent birds and an over-sized baby—a teenager, really—squabbled over something. Food, most likely.

Noah crept carefully through the wet grass, stopping every few steps to listen, willing the deer to be there. He thought he saw something move under the trees near the fence and waited, heart hammering. He smelled something on the air: a warm, musky, *animal* smell.

There was no sign of the deer, but there was something else. Noah knew instantly what it meant, and hope soared in his chest for a second: evidence. The deer was real. It had been here only minutes before. It had left a small heap of shiny black droppings. Unmistakably deer poo.

Yes! He'd got proof.

He hadn't imagined it.

And an actual deer—surely that would help them save

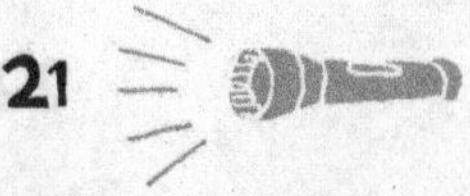

the Wilderness? If they could tell someone important . . .

The deer's sensitive hearing meant it had fled before Noah could see it. Maybe he could borrow a camera, take a photo of it, as proof?

Noah changed direction, and made his way uphill to check the horrible For Sale sign was still there.

But of course it was.

Stupid. How could it not be?

Noah shook the post with both hands, rocking it to and fro. The post had been hammered in deep and hardly budged.

He tried pulling off the plastic notice but it wouldn't tear. He kicked the post, and hurt his foot. He needed a saw. Or a match, to burn it down. And even that wouldn't change anything really, would it? The notice itself wasn't the real problem.

It was what it meant that mattered.

Noah checked the houses again. It was still so early no one else was up. The doors were all shut, the windows blank, curtains closed, as if the houses were asleep like the people inside. *Hurry up!* he willed Toby.

He gave the post one last kick and zigzagged through the

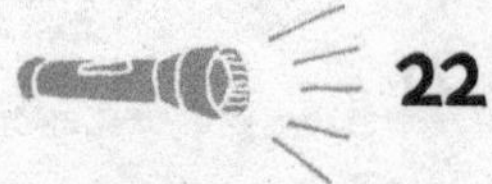

long grass, skirting a large clump of stinging nettles, downhill towards the dump, where people chucked old rubbish and stuff over the fence. He'd get on with building the first lookout.

No! By mistake he'd squished a snail. He hated hurting things.

He dragged an old wooden pallet out of the heap of rubbish, and leaned it up against a tree to dry off. He picked through the pile, finding more wooden planks half-hidden under ivy and bindweed, and he dusted off the woodlice and stacked the wood against another tree.

Now, he needed a hammer and nails.

He ran back through the long damp grass. The greenhouse had once belonged to old Mr Moss at number twelve, and some of his tools were still there: garden spade and forks, a hammer, nails. Mr Moss wouldn't mind. He was the only adult on the street who actually seemed to like the Wilderness. Last summer, he'd given Noah a book about wildlife. 'You'll make more use of it than me, Noah,' he'd said.

Noah tugged open the bottom drawer in the chest of drawers and put a handful of nails into his pocket. Most of them were rusty. He took the hammer from its hook on the back of the door, and picked up a spade.

Noah chose his tree: the tallest one, with no nest, where the branches were well spaced. He dragged the wooden pallet and planks to the base, and climbed up, carrying them one at a time. He chose a fork in the tree as the best place to build. It was hard work; only the longest nails would go right through the wood into the tree. The sounds echoed over the Wilderness. Surely that would wake the others up?

There. He hammered in a final nail and looked around.

From up here, he had a birds'-eye view of the entire Wilderness and the street. He'd see anyone coming. He could keep constant watch.

He checked up and down the street for the millionth time. No traffic. The doors of all the houses were still shut. No sign of Toby. No one but him was awake.

Noah couldn't stand it any longer. He climbed down from the platform, grazing his knees on the rough tree bark as he swung from the lowest branch and slid down the trunk, and ran down the hill to Toby's house.

He threw a handful of gravel up at Toby's bedroom window.

Toby's face appeared in a gap between the curtains, then disappeared.

The door at number seven opened.

'Toby!' Noah yelled. He ran towards him, tripping over his feet in his rush. 'Something terrible's happened.' He was out of breath, his chest hurting. The words tumbled out too fast. 'Wilderness. For sale. Building houses.'

'What? Slow down, Noah! Say again?'

'Someone's put a notice up, about selling the Wilderness. Building houses here.'

Finally, Toby did understand. '*Whaaat!* Show me.'

'Up the top.' Noah led the way. He was almost sobbing with the relief of sharing the horrible news with someone else at last.

Chapter 5

Toby said the words out loud, and each one felt like a heavy stone dropping into Noah's stomach. Instead of a relief, it made it worse, as if it was more real now Toby was reading the notice too.

LAND FOR SALE.

DERELICT LAND SUITABLE FOR BUILDING PLOT FOR HOUSES. PLANNING PERMISSION PENDING.

'What does pending mean?' Noah asked.

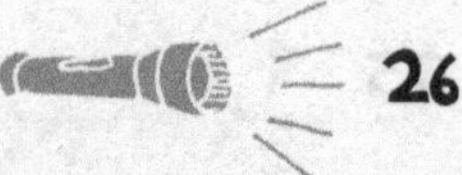

'About to happen.'

'We have to stop them,' Noah said. 'And I've got a plan.'

'What?' Toby said.

'I've already built a lookout.' Noah pointed to his wooden platform, high in the ash tree. 'And I thought, if everyone spreads out their dens, we can cover the whole area of Wilderness. Hiding places, to spy from.'

'Hmm.' Toby cupped his hands around his own head, as if he was holding his brain together. He frowned.

'What?'

'Shut up. I'm thinking.'

Noah's chest really hurt. Maybe he'd pulled a muscle, lugging the heavy pallet up the tree by himself. Or maybe it was something else. He swallowed hard.

'OK. Got it. Attack is the best form of defence,' Toby said. 'We'll make weapons. Arm ourselves. Paint our faces. Fight them.'

'But who are they, exactly?'

'Anyone coming on our land. Developers, builders. Council people. We'll attack them all.'

Noah thought about Toby's sharpened sticks. His home-made bows and arrows. Catapults. And then he imagined bulldozers and mechanical diggers and men with chainsaws.

Toby stabbed at the notice with a stick. He had that fierce, cold face that Noah recognized. Toby had been extra angry lately. Scary angry, sometimes. But that might be useful, right now.

'Maybe there's laws to protect wild animals,' Noah said. 'Cos I've definitely seen bats. Two, last night. We could tell someone. And we've seen squirrels.' He glanced at Toby. 'And now there's a deer.'

Toby didn't seem to hear. He kicked at the post. It stayed firm.

'How come the Wilderness can be sold, anyway? No one owns it,' Noah said. 'That's what my dad said when we moved in, so it was fine for us to play in it. And no one but us ever comes here.'

Toby started slicing the bark off the stick in thin strips with his penknife.

Noah knew he shouldn't have mentioned his dad. Dads were a sore point with Toby these days.

'What kind of deer?' Toby said.

So he *had* heard!

'How can there be a deer in the middle of a city?'

'I don't know but there is. I've seen it. And I found deer poo. I can show you.'

'Yeah, right.' Toby carved the stick into a sharp point. He held it out: an arrow, aimed at Noah.

Toby didn't believe him about the deer. Still, he had the proof. If he could find it again . . .

'We'll get the others,' Toby said. 'Start making weapons. First, we have to get rid of this.' He kicked the post. 'Destroy it.' His face was red and furious.

'If they sell this land and build houses, it will spoil everything forever.' He slashed at the notice with his pen-knife, sliced it and stamped on the pieces.

Noah joined in. He jumped on the fragments of the white sign and trampled them into the mud.

Together, they shoved and wrenched the post back and forth between them. Gradually it came loose.

Toby threw it on the ground; it landed with a satisfying *crash*!

'Good. Job done.' Toby wiped his hands on his jeans, and followed Noah back down the hill into the Wilderness.

They climbed the lookout tree and sat together on the high wooden platform.

'That's where the deer was.' Noah pointed.

'If you say so.' Toby stood up. He jumped on the wooden platform to test it, and made the tree shake. 'The lookout's pretty good,' he said. 'But now we need places we can attack from, all over the Wilderness. I'll start digging a trench. Big and deep enough for two or three men, with a roof. We can hide in there with our weapons, ready to launch a ground attack.' He climbed down the tree, took the spade from where Noah had left it at the bottom, and paced out a rough rectangle, right in the middle of the Wilderness. He sliced the grass and weeds off the top with the spade.

Toby dug savagely at the ground. He threw the earth into a heap as he dug down deep. The mound got steadily bigger. Noah watched him crashing around in the undergrowth searching for stuff. He came back with an old door, paint peeling off, which he tried out as a roof for the trench. He dug some more.

From the tree, Noah peered down anxiously for creatures that might need rescuing. But there were none. Not even worms.

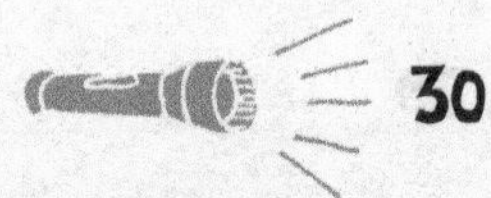

The colour of the soil changed from muddy brown to sandy yellow, and then Toby hit a layer of sticky clay.

Noah picked off a piece of twig and aimed it at Toby's head, to make Toby look up.

'Can I help?'

Toby shook his head.

'I'm really starving,' Noah said. 'I'll grab some breakfast and be straight back.'

Noah clambered down the tree and raced home.

Chapter 6

Mum was in the kitchen making toast and coffee. She had the radio turned up loud. She looked up as he ran in. 'Noah! Early bird! Hungry?'

He nodded. He poured out a bowl of cereal and drowned it with milk.

The news came on the radio. Only eight o'clock. He'd been up for hours.

'Dad will be at home while I'm at work today,' Mum said. 'No getting into mischief. And keep an eye on Natalie, please.' She poured coffee into a flask. 'You were very late in last night, Noah.'

Noah swallowed a mouthful of cereal. 'Mum, something

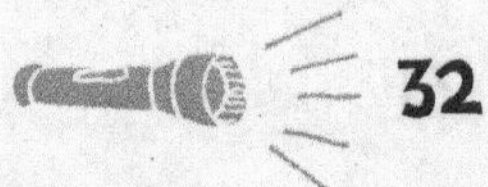

terrible's happened.' The words caught in his throat. 'The Wilderness is for sale.'

'Oh, Noah!' Mum stopped pouring for a second, to look at him properly. 'That's so sad. We didn't think it belonged to anyone, did we? So all your lovely games will have to stop . . .'

Noah shut his eyes, as if that would stop his ears hearing what she was saying.

'I have to go to work now, but we'll talk about it this afternoon, when I'm back. Yes?' She rubbed his back as she went past.

He blinked hard. He gulped down the rest of the cereal and cut himself a hunk of bread and spread it thick with butter and honey. He took it with him back outside, taking big bites as he went across the road.

At the edge of the grass he stopped for a moment.

He stared at the Wilderness.

Something was different.

That early morning feeling had gone. The sounds had changed. The dual carriageway down in the valley was an unbroken line of cars and lorries coming into the city. The hum of traffic was so loud it drowned out the sound of birdsong.

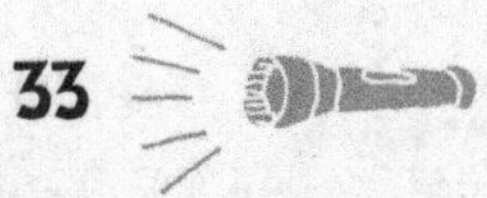

But it was more than that. It was as if already some of the magic was draining away from the Wilderness. For the first time ever, for the briefest moment, Noah glimpsed the Wilderness like a stranger might: an overgrown, scruffy patch of weeds and trees and bushes and long grass, rather than the magical, wild, beautiful place Noah knew it to be.

He blinked, to make the picture go away.

He stuffed down the last of the bread and ran through the long grass towards Toby's trench.

Where was Toby?

For a moment, Noah wondered whether he'd fallen into his own deep hole and buried himself. He peered in.

The spade was lying on the ground, abandoned, as if Toby had left in a hurry.

Noah climbed up the tree to see if he could spot him.

A white van was parked at the top of the road. A white van with green writing on the side and . . . Noah screwed up his eyes to see better . . . a picture of a tree. Something was happening: a man, arguing with . . .

Oh no!

. . . With Toby!

Noah scrambled down the tree and ran up the hill.

Toby raced halfway to meet him. 'That stupid man says he's come to cut down the trees!' Toby was ready to explode.

'No! He can't!'

'Obviously.'

'But who is he? A builder? Is it sold ALREADY?'

'He's some random tree man. Says he's following orders.'

The man shifted his feet. He checked his mobile phone.

Noah took in the steel-capped boots, the navy overalls and the bright yellow safety helmet. The chainsaw in the back of the van. Close up, he could read the words on the side, now. Tree Solutions. The man meant business.

Noah clenched his fists to stop his hands shaking. He was scared but he knew he had to do something. 'I'll talk to him,' he told Toby.

'Orders is orders,' the man said, before Noah had even opened his mouth. 'There's been complaints. It's not safe. The big ash trees near the fence need to come down.'

'You can't cut down the trees,' Noah said. His voice came out surprisingly strong and calm. 'They're *our* trees.'

The man coughed. 'Sorry, kids,' he said. 'Loved climbing trees myself when I was your age. But them trees have got too tall. Dangerous. Loose branches overhanging the fence. Council property the other side.'

He made it sound as if all this was entirely unconnected to the For Sale sign. But Noah was suspicious. It was too much of a coincidence. No one had ever come to cut down trees before. He thought fast.

'There's nests,' he said. 'You can't cut down trees with nests.'

The man took off the helmet and scratched his head. 'Well, I'll check that out, first.'

'You can see them from here,' Toby said.

All three turned to look. Sure enough, the crows' nests stood out clear: black bundles of sticks, the adult crows balanced on the edge.

'Just crows, is it?' the man asked. 'The law doesn't include crows.'

'No. Robins and wrens and pigeons and blackbirds and starlings and magpies and owls.' Noah listed them off. That was more or less right: he'd seen all those birds at one time or another, so logically they must have nests.

The man seemed to be actually listening, taking the nests thing seriously. So, it did matter. The nests were important. Phew. Lucky guess.

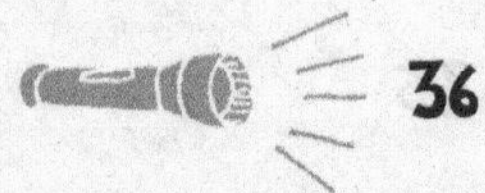

'I'll make a note of that,' the man said. 'And I'll check it out for myself. Thanks, kiddos.' He put his mobile phone back on the dashboard in the van.

Kiddos! As if they were about five years old!

Toby jabbed his stick at the pavement as if he'd like to do the same to the man.

Noah knew he had to stop the man getting anywhere near the trees with his chainsaw.

Holly and Nat had come outside. They were laughing and dancing about on the pavement outside number seven. Anil and Asha appeared too, and Zeke, bouncing a football. They still had no idea about the threat to the Wilderness. Toby or him had to tell them, somehow. And fast.

Noah had a brainwave.

'I'll go with you,' Noah told the man. 'Show you the way so you don't tread on the frogs and toads and beetles and *rare* creatures.' He laid it on thick, about the rare things, even though he didn't know if there were any. Under his breath, he hissed to Toby, 'Get the others, *quick!* and climb up the trees, to keep them safe. Tell them about the For Sale notice and everything.'

Toby nodded. He ran.

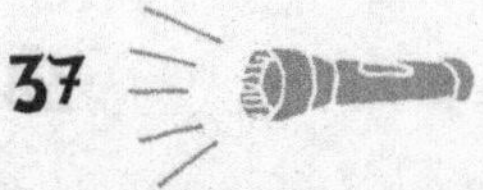

The man looked relieved. Toby was pretty terrifying, with his sharp stick and all.

'This way,' Noah said. 'Careful, there's rare snakes. Poisonous ones.'

'That'll be adders,' the man said. 'That's the only venomous snake in Britain. But they don't usually live in grass like this. Sandy heathland is more their thing.'

Duh. Of course Noah already knew that. But just his luck, to get a man who knew about snakes. He glanced back to check where Toby and the others were. It had gone very quiet. Good. Toby would have explained everything by now. They'd be creeping up the Wilderness next to the fence towards the trees.

He played for time. 'Have you ever seen adders?' He used his extra-polite voice.

The man stopped walking and smiled. He looked quite normal and human when he smiled. 'You bet I have. Loved 'em when I was a kid. Kept one in an old bath in the garden, me brother and me.' He chuckled.

Noah was genuinely interested now. And this was brilliant: the man talking meant lots of time for Toby and the gang to climb up the trees. The man couldn't possibly cut down trees with children sitting in them.

'So, how did you catch your snake?' Noah asked.

'Took time and patience,' the man said.

Noah nodded.

'We watched 'em, saw where they sunned themselves, in the bracken up at the edge of the woods near our house. Practised with a forked stick . . . got a female adder, beautiful markings . . .'

'Wow!' Noah said.

The man snapped to, as if he suddenly remembered where he was and what he was supposed to be doing. 'So, yours are grass snakes, probably. Easy mistake to make. Not poisonous. Walk on.'

Noah had to grit his teeth, to stop himself saying *of course* he knew the difference! He wasn't stupid. Not about wild creatures, anyway. 'Watch out. Nettles and boggy patch,' he said. 'Don't tread on the froglets.' He pretended he was stepping over tiny frogs, exaggeratedly careful.

The man picked his way past the nettles and through the damp mud, following Noah. His feet were clumsy in his big steel-capped boots. Any real frogs wouldn't stand a chance. He crushed the wild flowers underfoot without even noticing.

A magpie—black and white, long tail—flew past with a shriek, like a warning. *One for sorrow*, Noah remembered from the rhyme. He looked for a second magpie but none came.

Yes! Ahead of them, he saw the gang clambering up into the trees. Toby climbed highest; he stood on a branch, holding on with one arm to the trunk of the tree. Anil waved from the ash tree closest to the fence. Zeke perched on a forked branch in the old hawthorn next to it, his head dark against the green foliage.

Even little Nat was being hauled up a tree by Holly and Asha. They sat among the leaves like so many bright birds: Holly's blue top next to Asha's orange T-shirt and Natalie's yellow.

The man still hadn't noticed. He peered at a large black beetle at his feet. 'Haven't seen a stag beetle in years,' he said. 'Well, fancy that.' He crouched down for a better look.

Noah did the thumbs up sign to the gang in the trees. He waved at them.

Big mistake.

Natalie waved back.

There was the sound of a shrill scream and a frantic flurry among the leaves.

Nat tumbled from her perch. She must have let go of the branch, lost her footing. Noah held his breath as Holly tried to reach down to catch her, but she couldn't.

He watched Nat go bouncing down through the tree, squealing, all the way to the bottom.

'*Owwwwwwww!*'

Chapter 7

Noah sprinted down the hill towards his little sister so fast his lungs burned.

The tree man yelled and ran too, thudding behind Noah.

Natalie lay on the ground, sobbing and clutching her arm.

At least she's making a noise, Noah thought. Not dead. He knelt down beside her. 'It's OK. I'm here. You're OK.' He patted her leg.

'Everyone keep calm now,' the man said, all flustered and out of breath, as he caught up.

Holly jumped down from the tree. 'I'll run and get your mum.'

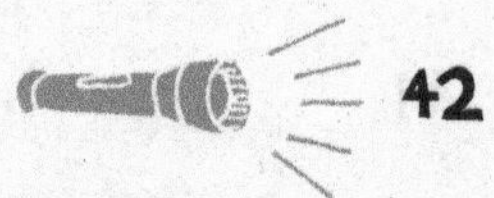

'Dad,' Noah said. 'Mum's at work.'

'I want Mum,' Nat sobbed.

'Which bits hurt most?' Noah asked.

'All of me! My arm!'

Her arm did look weird, Noah thought. Kind of sticking out, wonky.

Asha and Anil and Zeke had all climbed down now; they stood around Nat in a circle, staring, sombre.

'Nobody move the girl,' the man said. 'In case she's broken her back or a leg.'

Nat sobbed harder. But she sat up. She wiggled her legs.

'Don't listen to him. You'll be fine,' Noah said. 'It's just your arm, Nat.'

The man was in a total panic. 'I'll call an ambulance.' He fumbled in his overalls' pocket for his phone. 'Must have left it in the van! You stay still, kiddo,' he said to Nat, 'I'll be back in a jiffy.' He puffed and panted back up the hill, muttering to himself. '*Stupid kids*.'

Noah stared anxiously after him.

The sound of feet came thumping up the street. Holly and Dad were on their way. Phew.

Dad shouted something at the tree man as he went past.

He crashed through the undergrowth, following Holly down the Wilderness.

Noah saw his face, white and shocked.

He crouched next to Nat. 'OK, sweetheart, it's OK, I've got you. Now—what's the damage? Your arm, obviously. But anything else? Legs?'

She stopped crying so hard. 'My arm reeeally, *reeeally* hurts.'

'How's your head?'

'OK.' She sniffed.

'Back and neck?'

'OK.' Nat gave a last little sob.

'How far did you fall?'

'Not that far,' Holly said. 'She let go and slipped—we tried to save her, honest—'

'What the heck were you all doing in the trees in the first place?'

Noah's face went hot. Where to start?

'It's a protest, to save the trees,' Holly explained. 'That man wanted to cut them down. It's outrageous.'

'Yeah, so we're protesting,' Zeke said.

Dad scooped Nat up in his arms. 'OK. Listen up. We

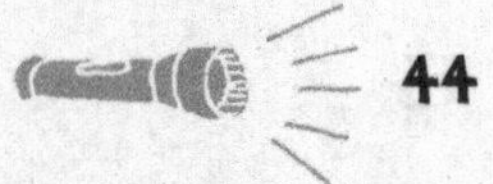

need to go straight off to accident and emergency to get that arm looked at, but you're going to be totally fine, Natty.' He frowned at Noah. 'You and me will talk about this later, Noah. *For now, stay on the ground*! *All* of you. Got that?'

'Yes, Dad.' Noah nodded. 'Good luck, Nat. Sorry 'bout your arm.'

Nat moaned with each step as Dad carried her up the Wilderness to the road.

Noah watched them go. He couldn't seem to move.

He heard raised voices—Dad's, and the tree man. He heard the words 'trespass', and 'advance notice' and 'council'. Dad was shouting.

The car engine started up; he saw Dad drive up the road, with Nat in the front seat. The tree man's white van drove away too, shortly after.

Noah unclenched his hands.

'Wow, her arm looked really bad, man!' Zeke said. 'I saw the bone sticking out.'

'No you didn't!' Holly was indignant.

'But she'll get a cool plaster cast. I've always wanted one of those!' Anil said.

Asha glared at him. 'Poor Nat, it must've really hurt.' She

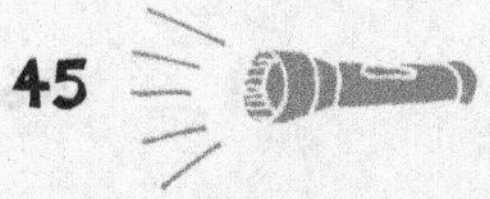

turned to Noah. 'What are your mum and dad going to say? Are we going to be in big trouble?'

Noah shook his head. 'It was an accident. No one's fault. Except mine, for waving.'

'You couldn't have known,' Holly said. 'It's just as much our fault, for making her climb up in the first place. Don't feel bad, Noah.'

Kind Holly. Noah was grateful. He still felt terrible.

But Toby, yelling from the top of the tree, was jubilant. 'Yay! Go, Natalie!' He punched the air. 'Result! We saved the trees! First round to us!' he crowed. 'Tree man, nil.'

'Poor Nat. You could show a little sympathy, Tobes. She's probably broken her arm.'

'Collateral damage,' Toby said. He climbed down the tree, light and agile as a cat. He jumped from the last branch and landed on his feet. 'That's what you get in a war. She's the first casualty. Cos this is just the beginning.'

'Yeah,' Zeke said. 'What's to stop the man coming back later today, to cut down the trees? Or tomorrow? Or the day after that?'

'We need a proper plan,' Holly said. 'We should have a meeting.'

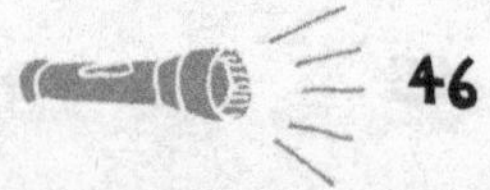

'There's laws about the nests,' Noah said. 'I'm sure of it. I'm going to find out.'

Toby took charge. 'OK. The tree man was the first invader. There will be more. Builders, property developers, council people. And the tree man is bound to come back. We have no time to waste. We need to make battle stations, fast. After that, we'll make loads of weapons. We need to be ready. We'll have a proper war meeting in the bramble den at three.'

Everyone listened as Toby talked.

'Natalie is the first casualty. There may be others. We will need to be strong and inventive and united. Us against them. From now on, this is all out WAR.'

Chapter 8

Everyone was busy outside on the Wilderness, making war dens. All apart from Noah, who had come inside to find out about nests and the laws about cutting down trees.

He sat at the kitchen table with Mum's laptop. There were pages of stuff to search through. His heart sank. Too much reading. So many long, difficult words. He wished he'd got Holly to help him. It was almost as bad as being in school.

The phone rang. Noah ran to answer it.

It was Dad. 'There's a very long queue in A & E. Nat's doing fine, aren't you darling? She's nodding. Brave girl.' Dad shouted above a background noise of squeaking trolleys

and bleeping machines in the hospital waiting room. 'You OK, son?'

'Yep,' Noah said.

'All right, then. I'll keep you posted. Bye, Noah. Take care. *Stay on the ground*!'

Noah went back to the laptop.

Dad kept phoning with progress reports from Accident and Emergency.

They'd moved up the queue. A man with a bloody nose had just come in. And three boys in a bike crash.

Nat was being taken for an X-ray.

Yes, the arm was broken. They were in another queue, for plaster.

No, the plaster would need to wait till the swelling went down. Temporary plaster today, and come back in the morning; Mum was coming straight from work to the hospital. 'And help yourself to some lunch from the fridge, Noah,' Dad said. 'Toby's mum's on standby if you need anyone, OK?'

Noah put the phone back for the millionth time and scrolled down another page of long words and difficult legal stuff on the laptop. His eyes and his head hurt now. The

words on the screen kept dancing about in front of his eyes.

Ah. Good. This bit made more sense:

```
It is an offence to cut down
a tree or hedge with nesting
birds.
```

Something called the Wildlife and Countryside Act and a European directive said so. Noah flipped through the next paragraph feeling a bit more cheerful, until he read the sentence that came at the bottom:

```
the official nesting period
is March till July 31.
```

Noah checked today's date on the computer screen: July 26. That only gave them five days. And that was just the trees. The whole of the Wilderness was under threat. At any moment the land might be sold, the bulldozers arrive . . .

The Wildlife and Countryside Act had a list of rare and protected species. Noah scribbled them down on the back of an envelope, ready for the meeting.

He found a bowl of cold tuna pasta bake in the fridge

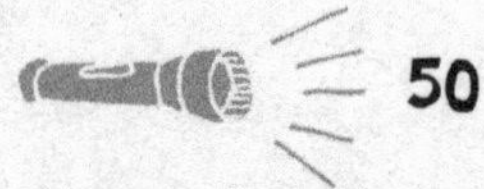

and ate it standing up in the kitchen. Now he was ready. He grabbed a knife from the drawer, for cutting stuff.

He ran down the road and across the Wilderness.

Holly was putting the finishing touches to her den.

'Wow, that's amazing!' Noah said.

'It's still a ship,' Holly said, 'but I've made it a pirate ship, now we are at war.' She hoisted the black-and-white skull and crossbones flag higher up a rope tied to the top of the broom-handle mast. 'Did you find out anything?'

'Yes. It's illegal to cut down trees with nests.'

'Good. Any news about Nat?'

'Broken arm; she'll be home later.'

'Poor Nat.' Holly picked up a plank of wood and started sawing.

Noah left her to it.

Over by the bamboo thicket near the fence, Asha and Anil were busy too, tying bamboo sticks in a tepee shape. Zeke had finished his den, a copy of Toby's trench but not so deep. The plan was working. There were places to hide all over the Wilderness, now.

Noah climbed up the lookout tree, to make sure there were no invaders. The tree man had not come back. He

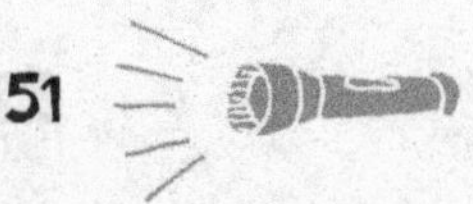

must have known about that law already. That was why he'd backed down. He'd wait till the 31st, and then he'd be back, Noah reckoned. In five days' time if not before.

Bramble tunnel clearance, next.

If you didn't already know, you'd never guess that beneath the huge jungle of prickly brambles was a network of tunnels big enough to crawl through, and right in the middle, a space where all six of them could sit. It had taken them hours every day for weeks last summer, and the tunnels were overgrown again.

Toby waved. He'd already started work.

Noah knelt down, feeling for the entrance on the opposite side of the bramble bushes. It was here somewhere—yes! He hacked at the strong green stems with the kitchen knife, slashing a way through. The knife wasn't sharp enough; he sawed and pulled at the thick stems and—ouch! He sucked the blood trickling from the torn skin on the back of his hand. Should have worn gloves. He needed a sharper knife. He backed out of the tunnel, and stood up.

It had gone quiet. Noah went up to the old greenhouse to find some old gardening gloves, and some secateurs or a sharper knife.

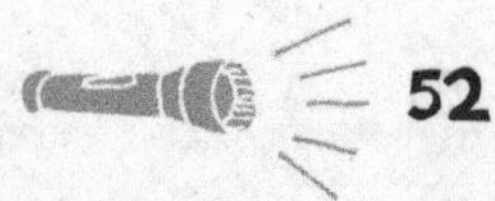

The car was back outside their house. The front door was wide open. So that's where everyone was! He heard Holly's voice, then Nat's. Asha squealed and someone laughed. Mum and Dad would be there too. Best keep out of their way a bit longer. And anyway, he had work to do. He slipped into the greenhouse without anyone seeing.

A spider scuttled under the bench. Noah crouched down to study it. Big black eyes; thick legs. Possibly a wolf spider. Noah stood up and opened each drawer of the wooden chest in turn, hunting for tools. He found an old seed catalogue with a picture of runner beans on the cover. From the second drawer he pulled out a leather glove—stiff with age but perfect for handling thorny stems. He hunted for its pair, the right hand glove, but there was no sign of it. In the next drawer he found a piece of folded paper, so old and soft it crumbled as he smoothed out the creases. The words were handwritten in a loopy old-fashioned style: the ink had faded but he could make out most of words:

Received as ground rent: the sum of two pounds and ten shillings and o pence, with thanks. Signed: M Treasure.

Cack-cack, cack-cack! Two magpies landed on the greenhouse roof. *One for sorrow, two for joy* . . . They strutted about, peered down through the broken glass pane as if spying on Noah.

Noah folded the paper and put it back in the drawer. The birds took off: Noah heard the swish of their wings as they flew away over the Wilderness. He rummaged through a pile of dusty sacks in case there was a knife hidden there, but all he found was a nest of woodlice. Defeated, he took the single glove and went back.

Toby's feet were sticking out of the bottom tunnel.

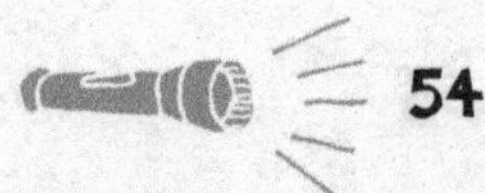

'Oi! Toby!'

The brambles shook as Toby wriggled out backwards on his belly. He sat up. His hair was full of leaves, his face smeared with green plant sap.

'You look like a soldier.'

Toby looked pleased. He spread out his hands to show off his war wounds. Purple blood stained both palms. A jagged gash went right up one arm from the wrist to the elbow, beaded with more blood.

Noah waggled the leather glove at him. 'Found this. But there's only one. And I need a better knife. Mine's blunt.'

Toby rummaged in his pocket and pulled out a small gadget. 'Knife sharpener.' He showed Noah what to do. 'Pull the knife back and forth between the metal bits.'

It made a satisfying squeaky sound. Now the edge of the kitchen knife gleamed shiny and sharp. Noah tried it out on a stem. It sliced clean through, easy as butter.

'Careful,' Toby said. 'It'll slice your fingers off.'

Noah winced.

'OK,' Toby said. 'Meet in the middle, yes? Team work. Where's everyone else?'

'Admiring Nat's broken arm,' Noah said, 'at our house.'

'Well, they should be out here,' Toby said. 'There's masses of stuff to do.'

He ducked back into his tunnel.

Noah ran round to the other side of the thicket. He stung his hand on the nettles a second time, before putting on the glove. He wriggled his way into the tunnel, slicing through the thick stems. Inching forwards, he rested on his elbows. It was hot work. He got into a rhythm: wriggle, slice ahead, to the left, to the right, above. The knife became a machete; he was slashing his way through a forest away from the enemy. It smelled of hot earth. He stopped for a second to give his hand a rest. He lay there, breathing slowly in the steamy heat. Now he could hear Toby, steadily moving towards him. Toby was humming something: the *Great Escape* theme tune.

'Oi, Tobes!'

'What?'

'Just checking. We're nearly through.'

'Cool.'

They could see each other now; just a few last bramble stems between them. Noah grinned. Toby looked like a

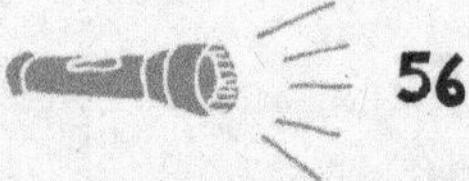

wild animal, his face streaked with mud and blood. 'Good idea, camouflage,' Noah said. 'We should all put mud on our faces when we attack the enemy.'

Toby nodded. 'I've been thinking about our weapons. Spud guns, water pistols, bows and arrows. Catapults: the hard little pears from that old tree make good ammo. Blowpipes would be good: we can make darts.'

'Blowpipes?'

'You blow the end of a bit of pipe and fire out a poisoned dart. Lethal. Saw them in a museum with my dad. Easy to make, with a bit of copper pipe, and paper darts with nails in the end.'

'Would they kill you?'

'With real poison they would.'

'But we won't have poison, will we? I mean, we shouldn't actually kill someone.'

Toby laughed.

'We could use plant poison, I suppose. Like, foxgloves are poisonous. Or some berries.' Noah thought a bit. 'But nah,' he said. 'We don't want to be murderers for real.'

Toby didn't answer for a while.

'In a war, anything goes,' he said.

Noah wasn't sure whether Toby was joking. Sometimes it was hard to tell.

Toby stood up. 'There's bits of copper pipe in the dump. Coming?'

Noah nodded. 'How long have we got before the meeting?'

Toby checked his watch. 'Half an hour. Long enough. I'll get paper and glue and you get nails. Make prototype darts to show the others.'

Toby was already running towards the dump.

Chapter 9

Everyone except Natalie was sitting on the old carpet in the bramble den, hidden deep in the middle of the thicket. There was only just enough space. They'd all grown since this time last summer. Zeke was the last to wriggle his way along the tunnel. He landed almost in Holly's lap.

'Oi!' she said. 'Get off!'

Zeke scrambled over her legs and squeezed in next to Anil.

'OK, everybody,' Toby said. 'Listen up. This is serious. We have a problem.'

'Houston, we have a problem!' echoed Zeke, in a fake American accent.

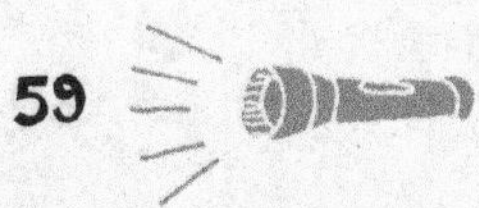

Everyone laughed.

'Shut up, Zeke!' Toby said. 'This is serious. OK. Listen, you lot. So far this is what we've done:

Step one, we successfully destroyed the For Sale notice. Step two, we scared off the tree man. But he could come back any moment. And other people may invade any time—builders, property developers, the council. So, step three, we all need to do shifts in the lookout tree and guard the perimeters—'

'What's perimeters?' Zeke asked.

'Edges,' Anil explained.

'And four, prepare weapons for the attack. Each den should have a supply.'

'Of what?' Holly asked.

'Spud guns, bows and arrows, water pistols—'

'And water bombs—we can set up buckets in the trees with ropes to tip the water on anyone who gets close.' Zeke grinned.

'Yep. And blowpipe darts. Noah?'

Noah fished in his pocket and pulled out one of the darts they'd just made.

Toby demonstrated with the copper pipe.

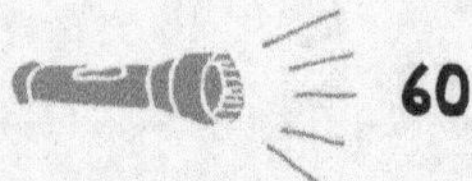

'Cool!' Zeke said. 'Give us a go.'

Everyone had a turn. It was harder than it looked. There wasn't much space in the den.

'Ouch!' Anil yelled, as Zeke shot him in the leg by mistake.

'OK, now everyone shut up and sit down,' Toby said, 'before there's worse injuries. We need to make more darts after the meeting. Who wants to help?'

'Me,' Zeke said.

'OK. But no messing about.'

'What else?'

'Tripwires?' Anil suggested. 'Man-traps?'

'What are they?'

'Like in Winnie-the-Pooh,' Anil said. 'The Very Deep Pit for catching Heffalumps.'

'Not exactly,' Holly said. 'Heffalumps aren't real, and Piglet got scared—'

'What are you two even *talking* about?' Zeke said.

'Never mind,' Anil said. 'The point is, we dig a line of man-traps along the road edge. Perimeter. Whatever. Deep trenches, like Toby's den, but you cover them up with grass and sticks so they're invisible to anyone who doesn't know, and then when they walk onto our Wilderness they'll step onto the grass and sticks which give way and they fall in.'

'And break their legs!' Zeke's face lit up.

'Well, get a shock. Sprain an ankle, maybe.'

'You're all so violent,' Asha said. 'There's other ways of protecting things, you know.'

Toby sighed.

'It is a *war*, Asha,' Zeke said.

'Yes, but we should outsmart the enemy, too. Use our brains. Like, find out about the laws.'

'I already did,' Noah said.

'OK, Noah's turn to speak,' Holly said.

Toby and Zeke were stabbing sticks into the earth.

'*Listen*!' Holly shouted.

'Birds' nests in trees,' Noah said. 'The good news is, it's actually *illegal* to cut down trees with nests in.'

'Yay!' Holly said.

'But the bad news is, the official nesting season ends in five days' time. July 31st.'

'Our nests still have babies in!' Asha said.

'Exactly,' Noah said. 'We know that. But we have to get proof.'

'I can take photos,' Anil suggested. 'And any idiot can see the nests with their own eyes.'

'It will take too long,' Toby said. 'And what's the point? If someone comes and cuts down the trees or bulldozes the land, photos aren't going to help. We have to fight.'

'Words can fight too,' Asha said. 'The pen is mightier than the sword—'

Zeke laughed.

'Shut *up*!' Holly said. 'Asha has a point. We have to show people how much we love the Wilderness. What it means. Why it needs protecting.'

'There's more laws,' Noah said. 'If you find evidence of Rare Species.'

'Such as?' Toby asked. 'Get on with it, Noah.'

Noah fumbled in his pocket for the envelope. 'OK. Here goes. Red squirrel. Otter. Horseshoe bats, slow-worms, great crested newts, some kinds of beetles including the violet click beetle, adders, dormice, dolphins, some kinds of moths and butterflies: silver-spotted skipper, swallowtail, wood white, small blue . . .'

Zeke had started giggling at dolphins.

Noah stopped reading.

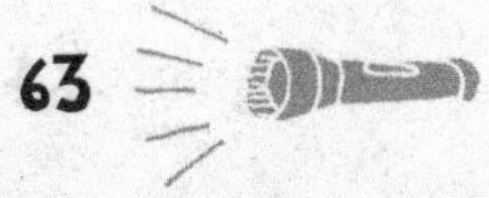

He thought of the deer. But that wasn't on the list. It wasn't rare, or protected, apparently.

'Finished?' Toby was fidgeting, desperate to get back in charge. 'Can we get on with the actual WAR plan? Listen. Zeke, me, and Noah make more blowpipe darts. Everyone get a stack of water pistols and buckets for each den. Spud guns and bows and arrows and anything else you can find. Anil, Holly, and Zeke dig man-traps and lay tripwires and booby traps. Prepare for imminent attack. I'm Commander-in-Chief. In charge of reconnaissance, mission control, communications, and everything else.'

Holly laughed. 'Yeah, right, bossy-boots brother.'

'I'll do first shift on the lookout tonight,' Toby said, ignoring her.

'I'll do early morning,' Noah said.

'Are we playing man-hunt later?' Zeke asked.

'No time for that. We'll practise attacking an enemy for real, instead.'

'OK. Meet after tea,' Holly said. A fat bee was buzzing round her head. She swatted it out of the way.

'It's a bumblebee,' Noah said. 'Buff-tailed. It won't hurt you.'

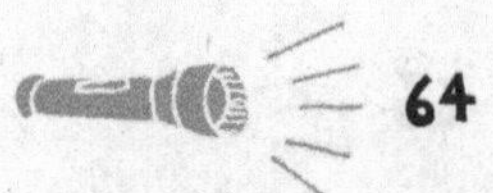

'I know that,' Holly said. 'And I know there are hundreds of different kinds of bees, before you tell me that, too.'

Zeke pushed towards the exit tunnel, squashing everyone in his way.

'Meeting dismissed!' Toby shouted over the squeals of protest. 'The fight begins!'

Chapter 10

It was nearly teatime. Noah couldn't avoid it any longer. He had to go home, face Mum and Dad, and see what state Nat was in. He trailed up the road. The Tree Solutions van hadn't come back, so far.

He practised blowing paper darts out of the bit of copper pipe. You had to blow really hard, and the dart shot out the end, nail first. His cheeks hurt. He picked up the darts and put them carefully in his pockets for later. Best not to let Mum see them.

Nat lay on the sofa, legs up, resting against plump blue cushions, being waited on hand and foot by Asha and Holly.

Noah groaned from the doorway. No one noticed. They were too busy paying attention to Nat.

'Hi, Noah! Look!' Nat held out her arm for him to see. 'It's a temporary plaster. My arm's too swollen for the real actual plaster to go on.' She winced as she moved the arm, for maximum effect. 'But you can write on it if you want, Noah.'

Nat was talking in her worst *spoiled princess* voice. Noah's heart sank even further.

The plaster was already decorated with flowers and tiny pink hearts and names.

Asha held out a selection of felt-tip pens for him to choose from.

Weird, Noah thought. And, *why*?

'How long will it take to get better?' Noah asked. He ignored the pens.

Asha put them back on the coffee table next to the tray of drinks. And cake, Noah noticed. Hmm. That was more like it. He took a big slice.

'That's *my* special cake,' Nat said. 'You should've asked first.'

'Sorry,' Noah said, through a large mouthful of lemon drizzle cake. 'Yum.'

'Three weeks at least,' Holly said, in answer to Noah's question. 'But we reckon Nat can still join in most things.'

'But absolutely no tree climbing!' Mum came through the doorway. 'Not for Nat, not for any of you. Nothing the tiniest bit dangerous.'

Noah prepared himself for what she was going to say next.

She surprised him. 'We know it was an accident, Noah. No one's fault, really. But please, all of you, be much more careful.'

Noah said nothing.

Mum gave Nat a glass of water, and tucked a blanket up over her tummy. 'You, madam, need to rest and let the painkillers get to work.'

'It doesn't hurt—' Nat began to say. 'That much,' she added. 'I'm very brave, the doctor said.' She lay back on the cushions.

'Faker!' Noah said. 'It doesn't hurt at all!'

'Stop teasing,' Mum said. 'Now, you come and help me in the kitchen, while Nat rests. Time to go, girls.'

'See ya later!' Holly said.

'Laters!' Asha echoed. They ran back outside.

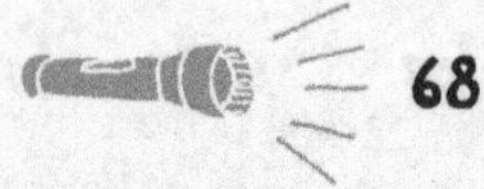

Natalie closed her eyes.

Noah followed Mum.

*

'Look at the state of you! Wash your hands before you touch anything!' Mum said.

At least she wasn't properly cross. He wasn't going to be told off after all. And she needn't know anything about his look-out . . . and he hadn't actually promised not to climb trees.

'All right, son?' Dad came in from the car and dumped two carrier bags on the kitchen table.

Noah helped him unwrap the pizzas and put them in the oven. He chopped up some fresh tomatoes to go in the salad. Mum and Dad went on and on about the accident and emergency department at the hospital, the queues, and the lack of staff, and NHS cuts.

Noah tuned out. He ate a bit of tomato and licked his fingers to slurp up the juice.

'So,' Dad said. 'What's all this about the wasteland going up for sale, Noah?'

Wasteland? But of course, he meant the Wilderness.

'Mum told me,' Dad said. 'We know you're sad about it, Noah.'

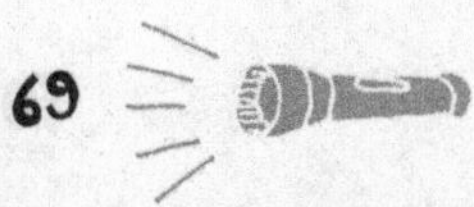

Dad looked at Mum. His eyebrows did that wiggly thing.

She looked back.

Dad nodded.

Parents were weird, the way they could talk without speaking.

Mum said loudly, 'I'm just going to take this clean laundry upstairs. Call me when the pizzas are ready.' She closed the kitchen door behind her.

Dad looked at Noah. 'OK. Let's get this straight. The land's for sale. You took down a notice, I hear—'

'Me and Toby. Mainly Toby.'

'You and Toby removed and destroyed an official notice. Which you should *not* have done. Noah. However, the land is still for sale, notice or no notice. I know you kids love to play out there, and it's a real shame, but that's just how it is, Noah. Some things in life we can change, some things we can't. Sad but true.'

Noah stared at Dad. 'Sad? It's a total disaster! Not just for us, for all the birds and insects and animals—there's squirrels and maybe foxes . . .' he nearly mentioned the deer, but stopped himself. Dad would never believe him. 'And lots of other wild things, Dad. And we *will* stop them building houses. You'll see!'

Dad frowned. 'Not by climbing dangerous old trees and getting hurt.'

'That was stupid Nat's fault. She let go and fell out. Duh!'

'She's eight, Noah. Not stupid.'

Noah was hot with fury. 'There are nests in those trees, Dad. It's *illegal*!'

Nat called from the sitting room in a quavery, pathetic voice. 'Dad? What's going on? Come here! I need you, Dad.'

'She broke her arm, not her legs! Let her walk in here if she wants you.' Noah was still spitting mad.

'She's a bit of a drama queen, I know. But thank goodness she's more or less OK. We can't risk a worse accident. And we can't have you being rude or aggressive to people from the council—or tree surgeon, or whoever he was.'

'I wasn't rude. I was really polite, actually. He was the aggressive one. He wanted to cut down living trees and kill baby birds. I thought you'd be on my side, Dad.'

'I *am* on your side, Noah. I'm trying to stop you getting hurt.'

The kitchen door opened. Nat stood there, the blanket

 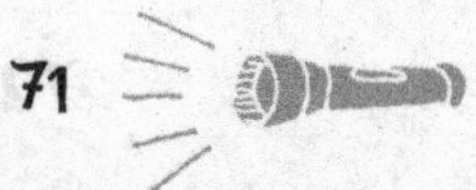

trailing from her shoulders like a cloak. 'What's Noah shouting for?'

'Go back and lie down, Nat. Pizza will be ready in a few minutes,' Dad said. 'We'll bring yours in on a tray.'

'I want you all to come in the sitting room with me,' Nat wheedled. 'I don't like being on my own. Pleeease? Let's be all together as a family . . .'

Dad sighed. 'OK. Pizza on our knees in front of the telly for everyone, this once.'

'You always give in to her,' Noah muttered. 'It's so not fair.'

Dad picked up the oven gloves and opened the oven door. 'Think about what I said, Noah. We don't want you getting into trouble. Or anyone else getting hurt.' Dad carried the hot pizzas over to the kitchen table. 'Right, Noah. Tell Mum supper's ready. And get cutlery and glasses of water for everyone, please.'

Noah called to Mum from the bottom of the stairs. He slammed the knives and forks on the tray. He stomped around the kitchen, crashing the jug of water down so some of it spilled.

Dad didn't take the slightest bit of notice.

Typical.

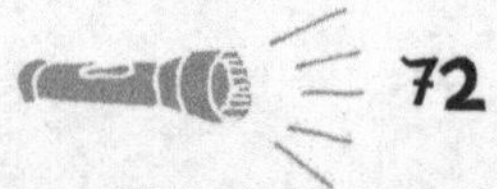

*

Natalie went to bed straight after supper.

Noah stopped off at her bedroom on his way out. He sat down on the end of her bed. She did look pale now, exhausted and somehow younger and smaller, tucked under her turquoise seahorse duvet.

'Sorry about your arm, Nat,' he said. 'Does it hurt a lot?'

She nodded. A tear trickled down her cheek. 'I'm going to miss *everything*.'

'No you aren't. Just tonight, and maybe tomorrow. Soon as you feel better you can come out again. Holly's made your den into a pirate ship and it's totally brilliant. You're going to love it.'

Nat sniffed. 'But I wanted to make it with her. The boat was my idea.'

Noah patted her feet.

'And it's not fair, cos just when I'm old enough to join in, the Wilderness is going to be ruined.'

'No it's not. We're going to stop anything happening to the Wilderness. That's the whole point. That's why you were up that tree in the first place.'

'But what if we can't?'

‘Don’t even think like that! We will. We’ve got a plan. Now I’m off to do war drill. If Mum asks, say I’m out with Toby.’

Nat nodded.

‘Sleep tight. Mind the bugs don’t bite.’

‘Don’t say that!’ Nat put her head under the covers.

Noah crept out, ran down the stairs, and closed the front door behind him.

*

It was dusk, the time of in-between, when the shadows were long and deep and everything seemed possible again.

Mr Moss was standing at his gate, staring up at the trees and the pink-and-gold-streaked clouds. ‘Have fun!’ he called, as Noah ran past.

Noah waved and kept on running.

Mr Moss didn’t realize they weren’t playing games any longer, that this was a deadly serious mission. War practice. Ready for the real thing.

Down on the Wilderness, Toby issued instructions.

‘OK,’ listen up. Me and Noah will be the enemy invaders. The rest of you have to stay hidden until we are close enough to attack. You have to try to take us by surprise. Get your weapons ready. But don’t actually hurt us, obviously.’

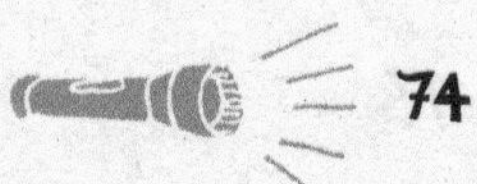

'How come it's always you and Noah?' Zeke said. 'Why can't I invade?'

'You can if you want,' Noah said. 'I'll do the lookout instead. I don't mind.'

Toby sighed. 'Can we just get on with it? So, me and Zeke are the enemy. We'll go up to the top of the street and wait round the corner so you all have time to get into position. Plus you won't know exactly when we're coming. That's more true to life. OK? Go! Action stations.'

Asha and Anil dived down to the tepee.

Noah and Holly set up the rope pulley system to get buckets of water up to the lookout.

'If this was a medieval castle, we'd be tipping boiling oil on their heads,' Holly said. She handed him a whistle. 'Blow this when you spot them coming.'

Asha was giggling in the tepee. She stuck her head out of the entrance to show Holly her face as she went past.

Noah laughed too. She'd plastered mud over her cheeks, and it was drying to a pale grey mask. 'You look like a ghost,' he said.

'Am I scary?'

'Very,' Noah said. 'Not.'

Asha stuck out her tongue.

Noah climbed up the tree. Everything was ready. It was just a matter of waiting for the first glimpse of the enemy. Any minute now.

He stood with his back to the trunk to get the best view up the street. He checked round to make sure everyone was hidden. It was deadly quiet.

The coloured prayer flags strung from Anil and Asha's tepee flapped in a gust of wind. Noah shivered.

His eyes hurt from looking so hard.

The wind dropped; an owl called from one of the tallest ash trees. A tawny owl, Noah reckoned. He craned round to see if he could actually spot it. No chance. And at that moment, he saw the shadow of movement. Zeke and Toby!

Noah blew hard on the whistle. Three blasts.

The sail on the pirate ship twitched as Holly got into position for firing.

Toby and Zeke swaggered down the middle of the street, hands in their pockets, pretending to be builders.

Now they were level with the tree, but still too far away. Noah reached for the rope, ready to tip the bucket when they got close.

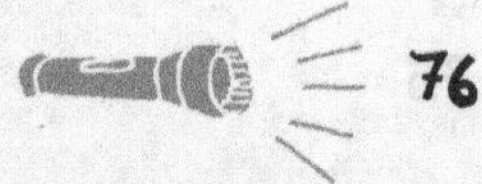

As Toby and Zeke stepped off the road and into the Wilderness, a volley of pellets rained down: Holly, with a spud gun in each hand, and a deadly aim.

'Oi!' Zeke spun round to face her. He hadn't expected that.

A spurt of water got him in the eye: Anil, with the big red and green plastic water pistol.

That was it. Zeke went ballistic.

He picked up a load of hard, unripe pears from the grass and threw them as hard as he could at Holly.

'*Ouch*!' She fired back. The tiny pellets of potato sprayed his face.

Anil joined in with a round of darts.

Toby was advancing towards Noah's tree.

Noah's hand held the rope steady.

Toby did his best impersonation of a tree surgeon. He wacked the tree trunk with his sharp stick, and at exactly the right moment, Noah tugged the rope. The bucket tipped.

'*Whaaaaaaaaaatt*!'

Toby was drenched. For a second, he stood there, dripping, incandescent with rage.

He finally found the words. 'Noah, you total idiot. It's a war DRILL. Not for real.'

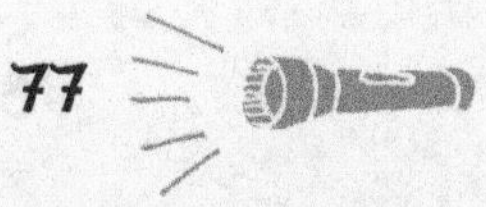

Noah grinned.

Toby had already grabbed the full bucket next to the tepee. He swung it, and water arced high in the air. Noah ducked too late.

'Water fight!' Holly yelled gleefully. She grabbed her bucket and joined in.

Only Asha stayed dry after that. She wouldn't come out of the tepee until all the buckets were empty.

*

Everyone went home to change into dry clothes.

Toby said they had to have another meeting, to review the drill.

'Let's have it in my den,' Holly said. 'Cos I've got biscuits and everything.'

Asha and Anil weren't allowed out again, so it was just her, Toby, Noah, and Zeke.

Zeke rubbed his face. It was still red from where the bits of potato had hit it.

'Sorry about that,' Holly said. 'I didn't know it would hurt.'

Zeke glared at her.

'The plan worked, though,' Holly said, perched on the deck next to the mast. 'No one will stand a chance if we can

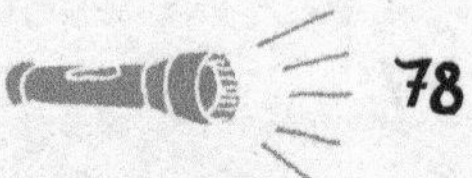

keep the element of surprise.'

'We need more discipline,' Toby said. 'So it's more organized. That was just a free-for-all. Stuff going everywhere.'

Holly sighed. 'It was fun, though.'

'It's not supposed to be *fun*,' Toby snapped. 'It's a war, remember?'

'We should keep the buckets full at all times. And we need a warning system, so whoever is on lookout can get everyone outside dead fast, if they come when we're in our houses,' Noah said.

'The whistle?' Holly said.

'Not loud enough,' Noah said.

'A drum? Empty paint cans? We could see if there's any on the dump.' Holly handed out more biscuits.

'We need to divide into two teams,' Toby said. 'The vanguard will attack first, to allow time for the others to either A, climb up the trees, if the enemy invader is the tree surgeon, or B, act as second line of attack, in case of the mantraps and tripwires being breached by, say, a builder.'

'I'll be vanguard team A,' Zeke said.

'OK. And me and Holly, cos our dens are nearer the perimeter. Noah, Ash, and Anil can be team B. Backup.'

'Now let's look for paint tins, for the drum.'

They climbed out of the ship and went to search. It was almost dark now, and hard to see anything properly.

Holly found two tins still half-full of yellow paint. 'Might be useful for making signs. Posters and stuff.' She put them to one side.

Zeke found an old television set. 'Wonder if it works?'

'Why would someone throw it away if it worked?'

'Might've got a new bigger one. With a flat screen. This one's ancient.' He picked it up in both arms and staggered with it over to his den.

'Keep focused on the job in hand,' Toby said.

Holly laughed. 'You sound like Dad.' She tugged at something metal half-hidden under a heap of grass clippings. A large rectangular can.

They peered at the label.

'Olive oil,' Holly read aloud. She shook the tin, peered inside. 'Empty.' She banged it with a stick and the sound echoed out. 'Perfect!'

Toby pulled out a second tin. Exterior masonry paint: white. 'This one's better.'

'Why, exactly? Just because you found it.'

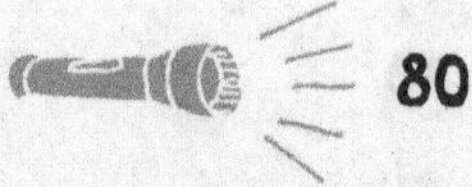

'We can use both,' Noah said. 'Even better to have two.'

Zeke loomed up out of the darkness. 'Two what?'

'Two drums.'

'Cool.' Zeke picked up a stick and beat a rhythm on the two tins.

'Ready for the night watch, Zeke?' Toby said.

'Ready how?'

'Warm clothes, food, torch, weapons?'

'How long will you stay out?' Noah asked.

Toby shrugged. He looked at Zeke. 'Midnight? What did you tell your mum?'

'Nothing. She's out. Dani's at ours, but she's watching films. She won't even notice I'm not there.'

'I'm off to bed,' Holly said. 'Coming, Noah?'

He nodded. 'I'll come down really early tomorrow, to do the first lookout.'

'Asha and Anil will have to take over from you. Toby and me will be out till teatime. I'll do the late shift.'

Noah nodded. He walked up the hill with Holly.

'Night,' she said, when they got to her house.

'Night.' Noah walked on up to number fifteen.

The air smelled different tonight.

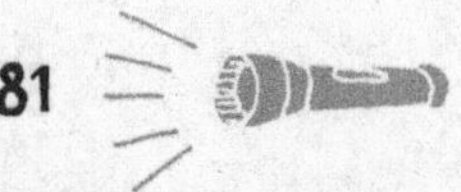

The first fat spots of rain began to fall. The tarmac on the road steamed slightly.

Summer rain.

Sunday 27th July

Chapter 11

The crows on the attic rooftop woke Noah early. They must be perched on the chimney pot; the chimney was like an echo chamber, amplifying the sound of their caws.

He pulled on boots and went out. First he checked up and down the street. All quiet, so far.

Noah waded downhill through the long wet grass. The ripe grass seeds left oily smears on his bare legs and hands; seeds and burrs and petals from the weeds and wild flowers stuck to his boots. He stopped to sniff the air: fresh and sweet after rain. The Wilderness seemed to zing with a vivid green light, and all the scents were stronger too. But there was no deer smell, and no signs of deer poo, either.

He went down towards the dump near the fence and stopped again to sniff. There *was* a strange smell here: not deer, but more like *barbecue*. Bonfire. Smoke.

Had someone lit a fire?

For a second, Noah burned with jealousy. He imagined Toby and Zeke crouched round a campfire, watching sparks fly up into the night, whittling sticks and mucking about together, without him.

He ran on. He saw now where the fire had been: a blackened circle of ground with charred sticks and a layer of white ash, under the shelter of the trees. It was hardly wet at all under the thick canopy of leaves. Three logs had been pulled round to make seats.

And now he saw other stuff: piles of empty beer and cider cans, a bottle on its side with dregs of wine inside, and more litter: cigarette stubs and old packets—a disgusting mess of it. It hadn't been Toby and Zeke's fire after all. Someone else had been here.

Who?

This wasn't builders or tree surgeons or anyone from the council. This was a different kind of invasion.

Quickly, Noah climbed up the lookout tree to survey

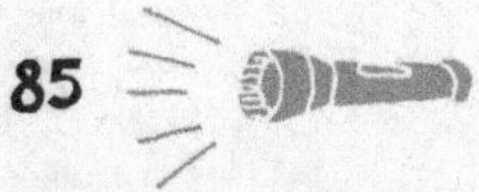

the scene. Zeke and Toby's battle station dens looked OK. He twisted round to check the other way. From the outside, the tepee and the boat both looked fine, too. Phew.

Further away, mist hung over the city and along the valley, following the line of the river and the canal and the railway. Why was it so quiet? Hardly any traffic at all.

Duh. Sunday. That was why.

Sunday was when Toby and Holly's dad came to pick them up and take them out for the day. Sunday evenings, Toby was usually in a bad mood.

When Noah's family had first moved into the street, their dad was still living with Toby and Holly. He'd helped them make a go-kart with some old pram wheels from the dump, and they'd done races down the street until Toby had had an accident, going too fast down the hill to stop or bail before he had crashed into the garage at the bottom of the cul-de-sac. *Never again*, Mum had said to Noah after that. *This hill is lethal.*

A sudden squawking made Noah look up. Two crows were fighting in the tree, flapping their wings and diving at each other, making a racket. Wind gusted through the

trees and showered fat drips down onto the back of his neck.

He checked the street one more time, and climbed back down the tree. He trampled the remains of the fire ash into the ground, and piled all the bottles and cans in one place. Yuck. His hands were all slimy and stinky. He wiped them on the wet grass.

The wind made the trees bend and sway, their green leafy tops heavy and full. Just ahead of him a tree groaned, a branch cracked ominously; seconds later it fell to the ground with a loud echoing *crash*!

Noah ducked. Lucky he wasn't underneath!

What was that? Something was moving among the mess of leaves and branch and twigs.

Noah stopped to watch.

He crouched down to see better.

Something small and black was struggling to free itself. It half-crawled, half-hopped.

A scruffy bundle of wet feathers.

A young crow.

Noah watched it struggle. He looked up into the mass of wet leaves and branches above, to see where the nest was.

The parent crows might be watching too, waiting for him to go away so they could rescue their baby. He backed off a bit, to wait to see what they did.

The baby crow—well, more a teenager crow than a baby; it was big enough to have fledged and have its flight feathers—hopped free of the wet twigs and then stopped still, its head to one side as if it was watching him. It blinked.

The bird hopped towards Noah. It didn't seem at all frightened of him. It opened its beak wide. It was hungry, asking him for food.

Noah rummaged in his pocket. He found a bit of old biscuit and crumbled it between his fingers.

There was no sign of the parent birds coming to rescue the bird. Maybe it was old enough to fend for itself.

Noah threw the crumbs.

The young crow looked at him with its beady eye. It looked at the biscuit crumbs. It did that three times before it gobbled them up. It hopped closer, opened its beak again. It squawked. *Aark*!

'Here.' This time, Noah held out the crumbs on the palm of his hand.

The crow looked at the crumbs, it looked at Noah, as if it

was working out what Noah was, and whether it could trust him. But it would not—could not—take the crumbs from his hand.

'I won't hurt you,' Noah said softly. He threw a crumb and the crow caught it and swallowed it down. It squawked twice, opened its beak again as if waiting for more. Inside its mouth was lined with pink.

Too much biscuit probably wasn't good for a young crow. Noah hunted about in the ivy, under the twigs and branches fallen from the tree. He found a woodlouse, and he threw that and the crow caught it and swallowed. Noah was so close up he could see its quivering throat. He dug in the ground with a stick and found two white grubs and he fed those to the crow.

A car reversed too fast down the street.

Noah raced back to the lookout tree and climbed up to check who it was.

The crow flew away.

The car had stopped at number seven. Blue Volkswagen. Toby and Holly's dad.

Holly and Toby came out of their house, and got into the car. The car drove back up the hill.

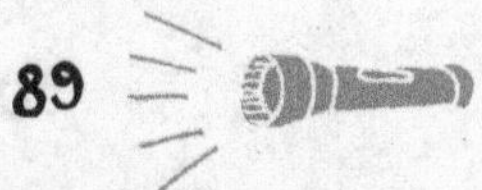

For a second Noah let himself imagine what it would be like, your dad not living with you any more.

He looked around to check for the baby crow, but there was no sign of it now. Oh well. He should be pleased, he supposed, that it was OK, not injured or anything.

He settled down on the wooden platform to keep watch. There must be two more hours at least till Asha came to take over, and he could have breakfast.

*

The street was beginning to wake up. Doors opened, people got into cars and drove off. Toby and Holly's mum came out and sat on the bench in their front garden with a book and a mug of tea. Mr Moss stood at his gate, watching all the comings and goings.

Asha and Anil ran out of their house and over the road to the Wilderness.

Noah waved wildly from the lookout. 'Your turn, Asha! I'm starving.'

Asha picked her way through the wet grass towards the tree. She stopped and stared. 'What's all this . . . this mess?'

'Someone's had a fire. Drunk loads of beer and stuff. I tidied up a bit.'

‘Bring a bin bag or something when you come back. It’s horrible.’ Asha climbed up to take his place.

‘There’s only four of us till Tobes and Holly get back at teatime. So we have to be extra vigilant. And we should refill the buckets and get the weapons ready, just in case.’

‘I’ll bang the drum if I see anything suspicious. Anil’s taking over from me. Then it’s Zeke, then you again. I’ve written a rota we can pin up, so everyone knows their times.’

‘OK. See you in a bit.’ Noah clambered back down the tree, jumped the last bit, and ran up the Wilderness towards the road.

Mr Moss was still leaning on his gate. He waved at Noah and pointed. ‘Made a new friend?’

Noah looked round. A few metres behind him, the small, bedraggled crow was perched on a low bough of the pear tree.

Aark! Aark! It turned its black head on one side.

‘Clever birds, crows,’ Mr Moss said. ‘That’s a young ’un.’

‘It fell out of a tree. It’s hungry. I gave it some crumbs.’

‘Looks ready-enough to leave the nest. Parents get sick of the young ones, turf them out eventually. Might even be starting a new family: new eggs to hatch out. But that young 'un will survive. It's taken a liking to you, Noah. Wait there a minute.' Mr Moss went inside his house. He came back carrying a brown paper bag. 'Here, you give it this. It'll get used to you, if you feed it regular.'

Noah took the bag. *Wild Bird Seed* was handwritten on the outside. He dipped his hand in; he scattered the handful of seeds on the grass next to the old greenhouse.

The crow cocked its head again, squawked, flew down, and pecked at the seeds. It flew back into the pear tree. It flapped its wings and spread its tail feathers. 'Aark, aark!' it called.

'See?' Mr Moss said. 'That's the ticket.'

'Wow. That's amazing!' Noah said.

'Keep the bird seed. Put it inside the old greenhouse to stay dry, lad. That way you can carry on feeding our friend Crow.'

'Thank you.' Noah took the bag into the greenhouse, and rested it on a dry dusty patch of floor next to the chest of drawers. Perhaps, he thought, he could explain to Mr Moss about the invaders. He could tell him about the For Sale sign, too. Mr Moss was the one grown-up in the street who really would mind about it as much as him.

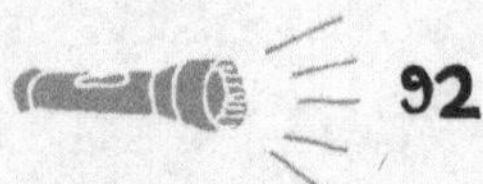

But by the time he came back out of the greenhouse, Mr Moss had gone inside his house, and Crow had flown away.

Chapter 12

Noah kicked off his boots and went into the kitchen.

Nat was sitting at the table, eating cereal with her left hand and making a mess of it.

'Where've you been?' she asked, through a mouthful of Frosty-flakes.

'Early morning Wilderness watch,' Noah said. 'Asha's doing her shift now. We might need you to help too. No tree surgeons or builders so far, but there have been other invaders overnight.'

Nat's eyes went big. 'Who? What have they done?'

'Don't know who, yet. No damage apart from a camp-fire under the trees.' He poured milk over a heaped bowl of

cereal. They never had Frosty-flakes on normal days.

'Greedy. Those are MY treat for my bad arm,' Nat said. She snatched back the packet.

Noah shrugged and carried on spooning them into his mouth. 'How is your arm, anyway?'

'*Much* better,' Mum said, coming through the door. 'Isn't it, darling? And Nat's coming with me to decorate Nana's flat this morning, aren't you?'

Nat nodded. 'Nana wants to see my plaster cast.'

Noah laughed.

Mum frowned at him. 'So, would you like to come and help too, Noah? I know Nana would love to see you.'

Nat pulled a face. She wanted Nana all to herself.

'No thanks,' Noah said. 'I'm busy today.'

'Doing what?'

'Stuff. With Asha and Anil and Zeke.'

'What sort of stuff?' Mum said.

'Oh, just dens and making things and mucking around.'

Nat made a sneaky face. 'They're making war things. Weapons.'

Noah fumed. But he kept quiet.

Mum didn't rise to the bait. 'Well, it's good to enjoy your

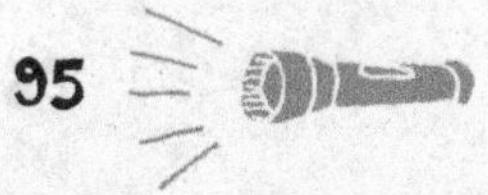

lovely outside games while you can. Take care, that's all. No sharp things. No falling out of trees. And Dad had better stay at home, in that case.'

'In what case?' Dad came in with a pile of old sheets and two pots of paint and dumped them on the table.

'Noah wants to stay here to play.'

'I'll be OK,' Noah said. 'The other mums will be around. Well, not Zeke's, but his sister Dani, and Toby and Holly's mum, and Anil and Asha's. So it's fine.'

Mum looked at Dad: a question mark.

'Just for a couple of hours, Noah will be fine,' Dad said. 'I'll come home at lunchtime, and you can come back with me to Nana's for tea, Noah. That way everyone's happy.'

'I've got to look for rare things in the Wilderness,' Noah said. 'It might take all day.' He thought fast. 'It's a special wildlife project.'

Dad nodded. 'Good lad. But you can spare an hour or two for your Nana this afternoon. End of.'

*

Why didn't he tell them the real reason?

Noah thought about that, after they'd gone and left him in peace.

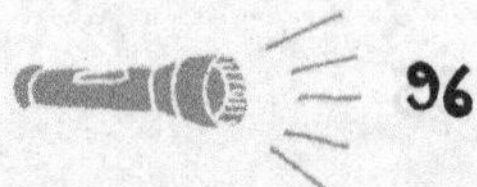

Because Mum would go off the deep end about war, and weapons, if she really knew what they were doing. Lucky she hadn't believed Natalie. She thought it was all a game.

Because Dad would go on and on again about not getting into trouble, and not getting hurt. He'd already said there was no point in trying to save the Wilderness.

That's why.

But he'd show them they were wrong.

Him and the gang.

Not Natalie, though. *Grrrr* . . . the way she'd tried to wind up Mum and get him into trouble! Typical!

Noah grabbed his list of rare species and Mr Moss's nature book and went to get Zeke. Otherwise he'd stay inside watching films and playing on the Xbox all day if his sister Dani was in charge, war or no war.

Turned out he was wrong about that. He found Zeke with Anil, digging a new man-trap next to the road edge, at the very top of the Wilderness opposite number thirty-one.

'This is the real actual front line,' Anil explained. 'If anyone like a builder comes, this is most likely the place they will first enter the Wilderness. So, this is where we need the first line of traps. That will give us time to man the dens, and launch an attack. Logically.'

Noah nodded. 'I'm going to try and hunt down something rare.' He pulled the list out of his pocket.

'Great,' Anil said. 'I'll get my dad's camera ready, just in case. Asha looked up that law: did she tell you? If you can get evidence, you tell the council and the government and wildlife people, and they make it a special place. And no one can build there.'

'An Area of Special Scientific Interest,' Noah said. 'I looked it up too.'

'Good luck with finding dolphins,' Zeke said.

Noah chucked a hard, unripe pear at him.

Zeke ducked. He threw it back.

But Noah was already too far away.

*

He went quietly through the long grass. He found a small beetle with brown wing cases and a shiny black head. He lifted stones to look underneath.

Aark! Aark! The young crow was back. It flew down from the tall ash tree and landed close to Noah. He chucked it a white grub – some sort of larva. Maybe he shouldn't have? It might be a rare grub.

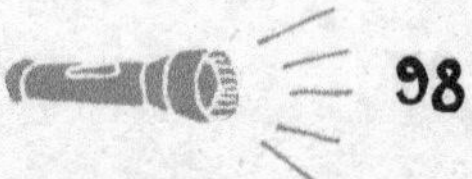

Too late. The crow gobbled it down.

Click. Anil was behind him, with the camera, trying to take a close-up of the crow but it flew back up to the fence and all he got was a blur of wings.

'Yell if you find something,' Anil said. 'I've got to go and do lookout duty.'

Noah laughed. 'Duh! If I yell, it will be gone in a flash.' He pounced on a small green grasshopper, and held it in cupped hands for Anil to photograph.

'Cool,' Anil said.

Noah watched him go.

Anil carried on snapping photos all the way over to the lookout tree.

Landscape view of long grass and wild flowers.

Close up of an unripe blackberry.

The wizened old pear tree.

Ash seeds, dangling like bunches of pale green keys.

Asha came to help him search. Noah was lying on his belly, close to the earth, studying a particularly beautiful, shiny-green beetle.

'Found anything?' she said.

‘Lots of lovely creatures,’ Noah said, ‘But nothing rare.’

‘What about the butterflies?’ Asha waded slowly through the long grass, to get a closer look. ‘Brown, sort of speckledy.’

‘Meadow brown,’ Noah said. ‘Nice, but not rare. There are loads of ants and hundreds of different beetles and lady-birds and grasshoppers and bees and flies. Millions. But nothing on the rare species list. I saw bats, the other night. Horseshoe bats are on the list. Only, it’d be hard to take photos of them, to prove it. And our ones visit, I don’t think they actually *live* here.’

‘Maybe it’s like Holly said. Everything matters on the Wilderness. Not because it’s rare, but simply because it’s here, living its life alongside all the other creatures. Why should one kind of bee or beetle matter more than another?’

‘But it does, if we want to make people see why the Wilderness mustn’t be built on and why it has to stay wild.’ Noah sighed. ‘Toby’s probably right. It would take much too long, in any case.’

‘What about the plants? A rare flower or something. Those pink ones?’

‘Rosebay willowherb. It grows everywhere. And so do

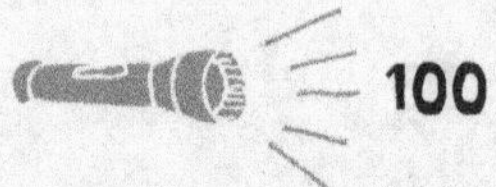

nettles, and brambles, and ragwort, and evening primrose. The tall yellow ones. And pink campion and lesser hogweed and old man's beard and meadowsweet and elderberry—'

'It's clever, how you know all the names,' Asha said.

'Not clever. You just have to look properly. Notice things. Mr Moss gave me his wildlife book, so I'm learning what things are called.'

'Should I ask my mum about that Wildlife law?' Asha said. She sat down cross-legged next to Noah. 'She might know more about it, cos of her job.'

Noah frowned. 'We don't want the parents knowing what we're doing.'

'Why not? They might help us.'

'They'll stop us fighting the war,' Noah said. 'Mine will, anyway.'

'My mum wouldn't like us fighting and the weapons and traps and that. But she might have ideas of other things we could do. I could ask some questions, but not say why. I won't tell her about all the war stuff. But there might be things about selling land, and planning permission. Stuff we don't know.'

'Maybe.'

'What did that notice say, again? Exactly?'

Noah shut his eyes, to help him remember. 'Land for sale. Planning permission—and another word. *Pen* something. Meaning, about to happen. And lots of other boring long words and long sentences I didn't really understand.'

'Pending? Was that the word?'

'Yes.'

Asha tilted her head, to listen. 'Your dad's calling you.'

Noah uncurled himself and scrambled up. 'Yep. I've got to go to tea at my Nana's. Will you be OK keeping watch? Toby and Holly will be back any minute. Tell them about the campfire invasion, yes? And we'll need to set up a special watch tonight, in case whoever it was comes back. I'll be home by then. I'm only going for tea.'

'OK. And I'll keep searching, just in case. Leave me your book and the list, and I can try and work out what things are.'

Noah was stiff from lying down so long. He trudged back up the hill towards Dad. At least there would be cake at Nana's. And he could tell her about the crow. She'd like that. And in a couple of hours they'd be back, and he could join the others for the night watch.

They had to be vigilant.

Danger lurked all around, now.

Chapter 13

On the way home from Nana's, Nat fell asleep in the car. Mum and Dad chatted in the front. Noah thought about Nana.

She'd been pleased to see him. She'd showed him the rooms Mum and Dad had painted in the morning, so the flat looked lighter and brighter already. Nana had fussed over Natalie's arm and made her feel extra special, so that had put Nat in a good mood.

Nana said she was making new friends already. People who walked past on the way to the local shops admired her pots of flowers in her front garden The next-door-neighbour was friendly too. It was a relief to have a smaller place to dust and polish and clean.

So, Nana was making the best of things.

Still, it wasn't the same without Grandpa.

It never would be, Noah thought. He remembered all the seaside holidays they'd had together. Grandpa had taken Noah out in a sailing boat for the first time. He'd shown Noah how to make a fire on the beach, and cook dough on sticks.

Nana hadn't listened properly when Noah tried to tell her about the crow.

Now, he was just anxious to get back to the Wilderness. Supposing something had happened while he was away? And they'd stayed much longer than Dad had promised, in the end, because Nana kept finding other things for Mum to help sort, just as they were getting ready to leave.

'Here we are! Wakey up, Natty Nat.' Dad slowed down and pulled up just past the top of their street, ready to reverse round the corner and down the hill. It was hard to find space enough to turn in the steep narrow street, so reversing was the best option.

Noah hated the feel of going back steeply, not seeing where you were going. He twisted round to look out of the back window.

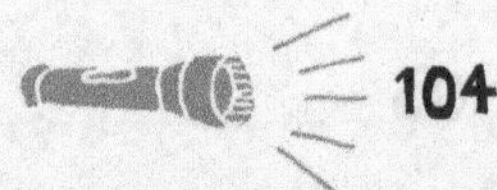

His stomach flipped over. An orange van, bigger than the white tree one, and with the words *Me and My Van* on the side, was parked at the top of the street.

Two lanky teenagers carried a sofa into number thirty.

Noah stared.

'New people moving in!' Mum commented cheerfully. 'And look, there's a girl your age. A new friend for you two. That's nice.'

The girl stood at the edge of the Wilderness, staring at the grass and bushes and trees. She turned as they reversed slowly past her, and when she saw Noah, she deliberately stuck out her tongue.

No one else saw, only Noah.

It was a shock. Unexpected, so they'd already passed her before he thought about doing the same thing back. In any case, she'd stepped off the edge of the road, and was picking her way through the grass, towards Zeke's den.

How dare she!

Cold fury washed over him.

Nat was rubbing her eyes, waking up. Dad parked the car. 'I'll make us some supper,' Mum said. 'You must be starving. You can't live on cake alone.'

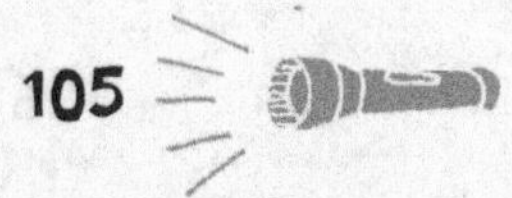

Noah didn't think he'd be hungry ever again. A mean, spiteful new girl in the street was the last straw.

*

'Did you see her? That new girl?' Mum asked Natalie over a plate of spaghetti with tomato sauce.

Nat slurped up the spaghetti worms from her fork. She shook her head. 'What did she look like?'

Mum looked at Noah. 'You saw her. Tell Nat.'

He glared. 'Girl. Ten-ish. Silly clothes. Mean.'

'Silly how?'

'Fancy. Girly. Not for running around in.'

'Hair?'

'How should I know?'

'Fair and wavy, I think,' Mum said, ignoring Noah. 'Shoulder-length. Lovely sparkly top and sandals.'

Nat seemed satisfied. 'I can make friends with her. She can join in our pirate-ship den.'

'Good luck with that,' Noah said as he left the table.

He heard Mum say, *What's wrong with Noah today?* and Nat answer, *He's always . . .* but by then he was at the front door, shoving his feet into boots, and out onto the path.

Zeke and Toby were in the lookout tree.

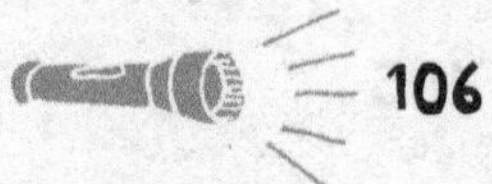

'You're late,' Toby said.

'Sorry. I had to stay ages at my Nan's.'

Toby nodded. 'We've got it covered. Because of the fire and the invaders, someone needs to stay out all night tonight. So Zeke and me are going to do that. You can take over in the early morning.'

Noah frowned. Toby was in a bad mood.

Sundays, he remembered. He wouldn't argue with him.

'OK. Good luck,' he said. 'Bang the drum if you need reinforcements. I'll leave my window wide open so I'll hear.'

He left them to it. He looked out for bats as he walked back up the hill, but he didn't see any. Perhaps it wasn't quite dark enough yet. Perhaps they'd only been there once, by chance, flying on their way to somewhere else.

He kicked off his boots in the hall, ignored the sounds of laughter coming from the front room, and ran upstairs to the attic.

Noah flung himself on the bed. Everything was going wrong.

There weren't any rare species on the Wilderness.

Toby was cross with him and being all friendly with Zeke instead.

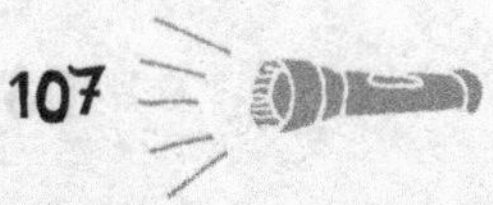

And now there was a new horrible girl in the street.

He opened the skylight window wide.

He listened: no drum, no voices.

The adult birds were scrabbling on the roof with their scratchy claws. Noah thought about little Crow, fallen out, or turfed out, of the nest. He'd feed him tomorrow, and get Crow to trust him, bit by bit. Make friends.

It would be Crow and him together against the horrible world.

Monday 28th July

Chapter 14

Monday morning. The clock said 7.25 a.m.

Noah shot out of bed, pulled on yesterday's clothes, whizzed down the attic stairs backwards, ran past Nat's and his parents' bedrooms bare-footed, shoved on his boots, and ran out onto the street.

He hadn't meant to be this late up. Typical: the one morning when it really mattered. Toby would go mad.

But there was no sign of Toby or Zeke.

Noah could see where they had been—they'd left an old blanket and two mugs and Toby's bow and a quiver of arrows. The water bucket was empty.

What did that mean?

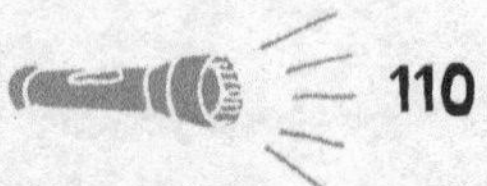

He peered down at the ground where the fire had been before. Was that new ash? Ash dampened by a bucket-load of water? Why hadn't Zeke and Toby stayed all night? Had there been a fight? Had he slept through the drumming signal, and had something terrible happened in the middle of the night?

Should he go and check they were OK?

But that would mean leaving his lookout post, and that might be fatal. Someone might turn up any minute now.

Noah hugged his knees.

Cars drove up the street, as people went off to work. The sun got higher, and warmed his back.

Noah worked things out in his head. His brain whizzed overtime.

If the tree man actually waited until the nesting season was officially over on July 31st, that gave them . . . Noah counted . . . three more days.

But he might not wait.

Especially if someone was paying him lots of money to cut down the trees.

The tree man must be connected to the Land for Sale sign.

Perhaps the land was already sold? And a builder wanted the trees cut down.

Or, perhaps it was the person selling the land.

And who was that?

A door slammed. Noah stood up to see better.

Toby and Holly.

Both were smiling.

Noah let out a big sigh of relief.

He waved at them.

Holly carried on across the road to her pirate ship; Toby zigzagged down the Wilderness towards him.

'You weren't here!' Noah said, as Toby's head appeared over the edge of the platform. 'What happened?'

Toby looked embarrassed. 'We stayed as long as we could. But it got really cold and Zeke was fed up. And there isn't room for two people to lie down. And Zeke was sleepy . . .'

'Did anyone come?'

'No.'

'What time did you go in?'

'I dunno. Really late. Like, one o'clock in the morning. No one was going to come after that, we reckoned. Not for a campfire and a party.'

'There's new ash. Someone's lit a fire.'

'That was us. Just a small one, to get warm.'

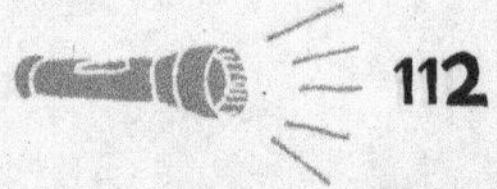

'I've been thinking. We should find out who owns the Wilderness.'

Toby looked at Noah. 'What good will that do?'

'We'll know who we're fighting, then.'

Toby nodded. 'Know your enemy. Good strategy. Fair enough.' He picked up the bow and set an arrow. He pretended to aim and fire. 'Phhee-ow!' He made the sound of an arrow in flight.

'Holly's on lookout after you,' Toby said. 'I'm going to set more traps. Tripwires, at ankle height.'

'There's a new girl on the street,' Noah said.

Toby didn't answer.

'I'll fill the bucket, first,' Toby said. 'Then tripwires. We found a load of cable in the dump.'

Noah lowered the bucket down on the rope pulley. It was a good system. They could use it for hauling other stuff up and down. Heavy weapons. Blankets. A food supply . . .

He checked the street again.

*

The sky cleared to brilliant blue. The Wilderness baked in the heat of a summer day. Even the birds and traffic went quiet. Anil was up in the lookout tree now. All the dens

were restocked with weapons. The tripwires were set. They were ready.

Noah buzzed with worry.

Nat had talked to the new girl. She'd found out stuff. None of it good.

She was called Feebee. 'Spelt P. H. O. E. B. E,' Nat said.

She was ten years old.

The teenagers who'd helped her and her dad move in to number thirty were her two cousins Spike and Gary. They knew people in the block of flats the other side of the fence and they already knew about the Wilderness, except they called it The Dump. They climbed over the fence sometimes and made fires with their mates.

'*Whaaaat?*' Noah yelled at Nat. 'It was *them*?'

'Don't shout!' Nat said. 'It's not my fault; I'm just telling what she said.'

Piece by piece, the evidence stacked up against the new girl and her teenage cousins.

'It's a disaster,' Noah told Toby. 'Now she's living in the street they're bound to invade again.'

The girl—Phoebe—was watching them from number thirty, half-hidden behind the cream curtains. Noah stuck his tongue out at her, and this time she retreated.

'We'll scare them off,' Toby said. 'We'll do it tonight. If they come tonight, that is. You and me. It'll be good practice.'

Holly trailed up the street looking hot.

The sun had made her face even more freckly than usual, Noah noticed. Her skin didn't get tanned, like his and Nat's did. This afternoon she was wearing a blue sunhat and a dress. She didn't usually wear dresses.

'Mum says come to ours for lemonade,' she said. 'And come out of the sun for a bit.'

Toby wiped his damp fringe back off his red face with the back of his hand, and left muddy streaks. 'OK. I'm parched. Coming, Noah?'

Noah followed Toby and Holly down to their house.

The lemonade was made with actual real lemons, and so sharp it made Noah's eyes water.

'Refreshing?' Toby and Holly's mum asked.

Noah nodded. His tongue had shrivelled up with the bitterness.

When she wasn't looking, they all spooned in extra sugar.

'Stay in the shade till it cools down,' Toby's mum said.

'You're all hot and bothered. We don't want you getting sunstroke. What have you been playing?'

'Nothing much,' Toby said.

*

Now it was late evening, time to get ready for the night watch. Noah told his mum he was at Toby's, and Toby said he was at Noah's. It worked pretty well, usually, unless the mums phoned each other.

Zeke hadn't told Dani anything.

'This is the plan. You stay on the lookout platform, Noah. I'll hide in here.' Toby walked over to his trench and kicked at the old door he'd put over the top, for the roof.

Or like a lid on a coffin, Noah thought but didn't say out loud.

The *thump* echoed off the fence.

'What if they see us?' Noah said. 'What if they're much bigger than us? Maybe Zeke should stay—?'

Zeke had turned to listen as a car reversed down the street and parked. A car door slammed. 'Mum's back. Gotta go. See ya. Good luck! I'll take over first shift tomorrow morning.'

'No one ever looks up,' Toby said to Noah. 'That's what's

so brilliant. You'll be safe.'

Noah wasn't convinced.

'It will be good practice,' Toby said. 'Like the war drill, but with a proper enemy this time.'

'So maybe we should wait and get everyone to do it—' Noah tried to say.

But Toby was already climbing into his trench. 'We need a signal system,' he said, as he lifted the door, 'but it can't be the drum. It has to be something they won't suspect. Owl hoots is better. Two means someone's coming. Three means, prepare weapons for attack. Four is *Fire!* But it might be a long wait. They probably won't even show up. Five hoots means we're giving up for the night. Don't do anything until I give orders.' He lowered the door the rest of the way.

You'd never guess anyone was hidden under that door.

Noah gulped. At least he wasn't going to be stuck in a trench in the dark like Toby, half-buried underground. He shoved his torch in his pocket and climbed his tree.

Up,

up,

up.

Chapter 15

Voices. Laughter. Footsteps.

Noah sat upright to listen better. He'd waited so long he'd thought no one was ever going to come. He'd almost fallen asleep. Now, he was instantly wide awake, alert.

The footsteps came closer. Loud whispers, and giggles, the clink of glass.

Two muffled owl hoots floated up from Toby's trench.

Noah peered down through the branches.

The fence shook as someone heaved their body up, perching astride the top for a second before half-falling, half-clambering awkwardly down and landing with a thud.

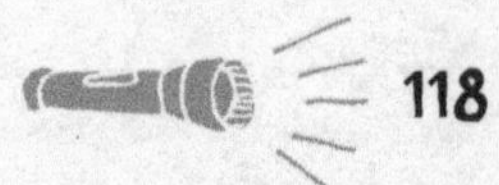

Noah could see her now: a tall girl with long hair. Another girl and three boys followed after her, swearing and giggling. Which ones were Phoebe's cousins? He couldn't tell in the dark.

Noah's mouth went dry. Supposing they saw him? He shrank back against the tree, trying not to make a sound. But it soon became obvious the teenagers were only interested in each other. And they had absolutely no idea they were being watched.

Were they drunk? They stumbled about, tripping over things. Noah heard the scratch of a match being lit, smelled smoke. He heard the hiss of cans being opened. One of the girls asked for a bottle opener and someone else laughed.

Noah wrinkled up his nose at the burning smell. Normally he loved to watch a fire, but this one seemed menacing and dangerous. What if a spark set fire to the trees? His mind rushed away, seeing threat and danger everywhere. He put one hand on the rope, ready to tip the water bucket.

'*Those kids might have left a penknife in that wigwam*,' one of the boys shouted.

Noah shivered.

The teenagers crashed their way downhill towards Ash

and Anil's den, trampling on stuff and laughing as if it was all a joke. Noah couldn't see them now. Were they trashing the den, tearing down the beautiful prayer flags and stealing stuff?

What was Toby waiting for? Noah strained to hear owl hoots.

Someone shrieked: they'd tripped over one of the wires!

Good. Served them right.

'What the—!' A loud jangling of bells rang out—and then another scream, as someone stepped in the boggy patch. 'My feet are soaked! And it stinks!'

Still no order came from Toby.

Noah couldn't stand it any longer. He grabbed the blow-pipe and lowered himself down, branch by branch. He jumped the last bit.

Toby's trench door-roof moved back, and Toby's head emerged. 'What are you *doing*? Quick! Get in!'

Toby dragged the door back over them. 'I didn't give the signal, you idiot.'

'They're wrecking Asha and Anil's den. We've got to stop them.'

'*Not yet*! I've worked it all out. We wait for them to get

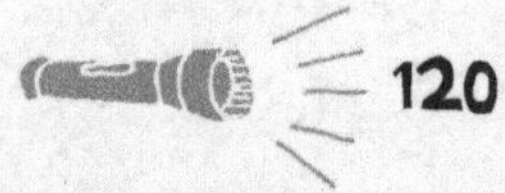

even more drunk and silly, and then we leap out, yelling our heads off, firing, and scare them witless.'

'But there's five of them. All bigger than us,' Noah hissed back. 'We should wait for another night, with Zeke and the others—'

'Seize the moment,' Toby said. 'We can do this, Noah!'

'Shshh! They're coming back!'

Heavy footsteps, more giggling. The sound of logs being dragged. More larking about.

Noah peered out of his spyhole: they were sitting round the fire now, swigging from the bottle, and chucking stuff which made the flames leap and small explosions pop and fizzle.

Noah tried to stretch his legs out. He shifted position. He was stiff from being scrunched up in the tight space. 'My legs are going to sleep!' Noah whispered.

'In a minute,' Toby whispered back, 'we push the door up, scramble out, yell, and chase them. Got your weapons? I've got my spear. The water pistol's loaded.'

'Toby—'

'Sshh!'

It went quiet outside.

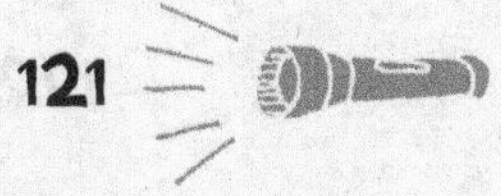

'Let's check again.' Toby pushed up the door, just enough for them both to peer out.

The teenagers were slumped round the fire. It had burned low, to glowing embers. Cans and wrappers and empty bottles lay abandoned on the ground.

Were they asleep?

No. One of the girls leaned against a weedy-looking boy—Spike? Or Gary?—and he started kissing her.

Yuck! Mega yuck.

Toby quickly lowered the door.

They sat in silence for ages.

'OK. On the count of five,' Toby finally said. 'You ready?'

No! Noah thought.

'Yes,' he said aloud. He didn't want Toby to know he was afraid.

'Five, four, three, two, one—*zero*!'

Toby shoved. The door toppled back and crashed onto the ground.

Noah kicked into action. He grabbed the water pistol and howled—part wolf-howl, part lion-roar.

Toby yelled his own peculiar blood-curdling battle cry as he ran, brandishing his stick-spear like a prehistoric caveman.

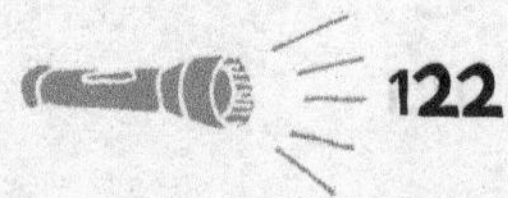

The teenagers scrambled up, yelling and swearing. They staggered towards the fence, tripping over each other in their hurry, in the dark. They screamed and swore, hysterical.

'What is it?' someone shrieked.

'I'm never coming here again!'

'Whose stupid idea was this anyway?'

They pushed and shoved each other, desperate to be first over the fence. The ponytail girl caught her T-shirt on the fence; there was a loud ripping sound as she tore it free. She threw herself over the top after the others, thumped down the other side, and ran up the path towards the flats.

Noah stopped yelling. He scrabbled over the dump and peered through the gaps in the fence but he couldn't see a thing. He pulled himself up the fence to get a look over the top.

Toby grabbed him down. 'Are you mad? If they look back and see us we're *meat*!'

But the teenagers were running away, their footsteps echoing off the tarmac, voices fading into the distance.

Noah followed Toby up through the damp grass of the Wilderness. His legs were shaking. But then he thought of those scared faces, the pushing and shoving bodies, each

trying to get over the fence first . . . and suddenly he began to laugh.

Now he'd started, he couldn't stop. He laughed so much he was nearly sick. He doubled over, laughter bubbling up and spilling over.

Toby was laughing too, now.

'We did it!' Toby punched the air.

'Yeah! They were terrified!'

'Thought we were zombies or ghosts!'

'Or monsters. Wild animals.'

'Didn't think it would be so easy!'

'Didn't you?' Noah looked at Toby's mud-smeared face and glittering eyes, at the way he was still jiggling from one foot to another, fizzing with adrenaline. Had Toby been scared, too?

'Let's stay out all night,' Toby said. 'Make our own fire!'

Noah hesitated for a second. 'I can't. My mum would go mad. But another night, yeah.'

Toby looked totally deflated, suddenly. All the fizz had gone out of him.

'How about tomorrow night, Tobes? We can bring food to cook and everyone can join in, yeah?'

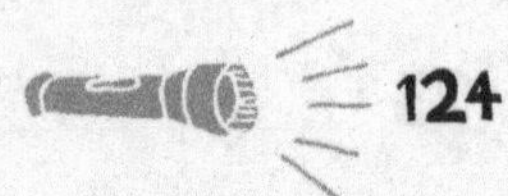

Toby didn't answer.

'It was brilliant, what we just did.' Noah said. 'Really worked.'

Toby gave no sign he was listening.

Toby was just so *difficult*, sometimes.

Tiredness flooded through Noah. 'I'm going home,' he said.

He looked back once.

Toby was still standing where he'd left him, perched on the edge of the Wilderness, a dark silhouette slipping back into shadow.

Tuesday 29th July

Chapter 16

Tuesday morning.

Noah had slept in late. He hated doing that. He must have been extra tired-out after last night.

Dad was busy at the computer. He looked up briefly as Noah came into the kitchen. 'All right, son? Another beautiful summer's day.'

'Where's Mum?'

'Taken Nat for her hospital appointment. Get yourself some breakfast.'

Noah shovelled down cereal in big gulps and put his bowl in the sink.

*

Zeke was on lookout.

Something was happening down at the tepee. Noah ran to see what.

Asha was kneeling on the ground gathering up her things. Stuff was scattered all over the mud outside the den—bits of paper, torn from a notebook, a cup, a rose-pattern tin with its lid broken off.

Noah stared.

Those teenagers. Last night. This.

'I'm really sorry,' he said. 'I wish we'd stopped them earlier.'

Asha was holding back tears. Her beads had been thrown all over the ground. She'd made them herself from the clay in the boggy patch, painted each one.

Noah helped her pick them up.

She smoothed the crumpled pages someone had deliberately torn from her diary. 'How could anyone do such a mean thing?'

Noah didn't know what to say.

He thought of Phoebe. FeeBee.

Her cousins. Gary and Spike.

Perhaps *mean* ran in the family. Like brown eyes, or freckles, or being good at sport.

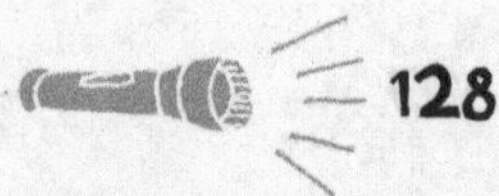

'My pretty gold bowl's missing,' Asha said. 'And the bell.'

They searched together among the grass and weeds around the den, but all they found were more of the clay beads, scattered as if someone had dropped them as they ran up the hill.

Noah couldn't imagine those teenagers stealing that kind of stuff, somehow. He wondered . . . had someone else been down here, early this morning?

Someone who liked pretty things . . .

Three magpies flew low across the wilderness, wings outstretched, chattering to each other.

'Toby told us what happened last night,' Zeke called down from the tree. 'Good job, Noah!'

'They won't be coming back! They were dead scared,' Noah shouted back.

'Where *is* Toby?'

'Dunno,' Anil said. 'He was here first thing, but he had to go back home. Holly too. Family stuff.'

'What were they like?' Asha asked Noah. 'How old? Girls or boys?'

'Both. fifteen, sixteen? Hard to tell, in the dark. Five of them. Big.'

‘Were you scared?’

Noah glanced at Zeke and Anil, to check they couldn’t hear. ‘A bit,’ he said, ‘at first.’

Asha nodded. She sorted the pages from her diary into the right order, and mended the torn ones with sticky tape. ‘I found out some things,’ she told Noah. ‘I asked Mum questions. Don’t worry, I didn’t tell her anything about the war.’

‘And?’

‘Planning permission. That’s the important bit of that notice you and Toby tore up. You have to get permission from the council before you can build anything. And there’s a meeting where it gets talked about and they decide yes or no. And anyone can go to the meeting and object—say why they shouldn’t build there. And also, they have to tell the people living nearby, in a letter, and that’s us. And they haven’t.’

Noah’s brain whirred.

‘So, what does that mean?’

Asha looked up from her pages. She seemed very grown up and serious. ‘So, no one has actually got planning permission yet, obviously. That’s why it said “pending”. We can

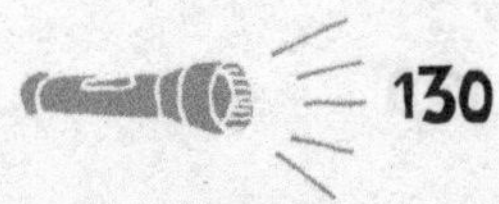

find out when the meeting is, and go along and object.'

'Have you told the others?'

'Not yet. I wanted you to know first. Cos you actually listen. Toby just wants to fight everyone.'

Noah nodded.

'Anyway, we should prepare evidence, ready for going to that meeting when it happens. So, Anil taking photos of The Wilderness is a really good idea—to show everyone how lovely it is. That's what I think. And we should go on looking for rare species. Bats would be good. Or newts.'

'We could make a pond,' Noah said. 'And some newts might move in.'

He thought for a bit.

'But we need all the other stuff too. The traps and the weapons, and the lookout and everything. Toby's right about that. We have to fight to keep the Wilderness safe.'

*

Noah sat on the wooden platform for the lunchtime shift in the lookout, planning how to make a pond, to get rare newts.

There was no sign of Toby or Holly, and everyone else had gone inside for lunch.

A flurry of leaves made him look up.

The small scruffy crow landed two branches above his head.

'Hello again, Crow!'

Aark aark!

It was definitely getting more confident. Following him, almost. Noah rummaged in his pocket for old seed from yesterday, and held it out on the palm of his hand for Crow.

The bird cocked its head on one side. It hopped down a branch.

'Come on,' Noah said. 'I won't hurt you.' He waited, patiently, with his hand held out.

Finally the crow plucked up courage and landed beside him on the wooden platform, and pecked the seed from his hand. The beak was sharp, stabbing at the seed. Noah held his breath as the crow ate it all.

Noah fished in his pocket but there was no more seed. 'I'll get you some.' He checked up the street. Should be OK to leave his post for just one minute. He clambered down and ran to the greenhouse.

The bird flew ahead of him and perched at the top of the pear tree. *Caw, Caw*, it croaked, an echo of the adult birds in the tall trees.

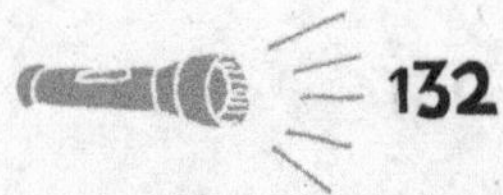

The new girl — Phoebe — was standing on the kerb outside number thirty. She was holding something, he couldn't see what.

Noah scowled at her.

She glared back, as if she was daring him to say something.

Noah pushed open the greenhouse door. He took a handful of seed for Crow. He crouched for a while in that peaceful, still space, trying to work out what to do about the girl.

Why did she bother him so much?

Caaw! The crow hopped along the greenhouse roof, looking down at him through the glass. Clever bird. It knew where the food was kept.

Noah sat down with his legs stretched out, and held out the handful of seed. He waited to see what Crow would do.

Noah smiled as the bird flew down and landed in an awkward flop. Crow was still learning about flight, and balance, and distance. 'Here,' he said. 'Come and get your food.'

Crow hopped to the open doorway. He hovered at the threshold, all the time checking around, his eyes darting, his head on one side, alert to danger.

A sudden flurry of movement caught Noah's eye.

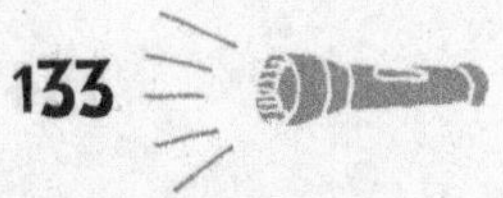

Crow flew off in alarm.

The girl ran down the hill in her silly sparkly shoes. Noah watched her stop near Holly and Nat's pirate ship. Holly hadn't come out yet this morning, and Nat was at the hospital with Mum.

He could hardly believe what he was seeing.

Phoebe walked through the long grass to the side of the pirate ship den, climbed in, and sat down.

Chapter 17

Rule number one of dens: do not go into someone else's den unless they are your best friend and say you can. Except in an emergency. Everyone knows that.

Not Phoebe, evidently.

Unless . . .

Had Nat said she could? When she was finding things out, yesterday?

It made him hesitate.

Just for a second.

Cos there she was, pulling stuff out of a tin Holly and Nat had stashed in the bow.

Noah ran down the hill.

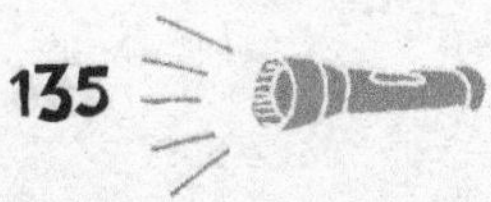

‘Oi, you can’t do that!’ he told her.

‘Who says?’ The girl stared at him, then turned her attention back to the roll of paper she’d taken out.

‘I do. That’s my sister’s stuff. Her map.’

‘A pirate treasure map? What is she, a baby?’

Noah went hot all over. ‘She’s eight. Natalie. You talked to her yesterday. And it’s pretty good, that map. Put it back. Get out of her boat.’

The girl did everything extra slowly, as if it was what she was choosing to do, rather than because Noah told her to.

‘Make your own den, if you want,’ Noah said.

The girl screwed up her nose. ‘Why would I do that?’

Noah didn’t even begin to explain. He was staring at the other thing she held in her hand.

A small metal bell.

He went hot all over.

‘You stole the bell!’ he said. ‘Unbelievable! Put it right back immediately. That’s Asha’s.’

The girl looked at him and for a second he glimpsed something else in her eyes—not mean, but sad, or frightened. But she covered it up quickly. ‘I found it on the grass,’ she said. ‘Finders keepers.’

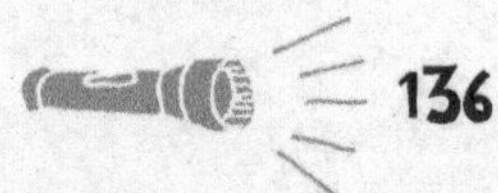

‘No,’ Noah said. ‘Not here, on our land. That’s Asha’s bell, and someone—some horrible people—trashed her den last night and that’s why the bell was on the grass. Give it back.’

Very slowly, with her eyes down, she climbed over the wooden planks, out of the ship den. She thrust the bell into his hand as she walked past without saying anything.

The bell was warm, as if she had been holding onto it for a long time.

Noah watched her trail slowly up the street. She looked so out of place, with her thin arms and white top and pink skirt. Her skin was extra pale, as if she’d never played outside in the sun ever. He watched her go right up to the top of the street and inside number thirty.

That was the third time he’d been brave and stood up for what was right. But this time he didn’t feel so good.

Where was Holly? She was good at this stuff. She’d know what to do now.

But neither Holly nor Toby had come outside all morning. Their front door stayed firmly shut.

*

Back on the wooden platform, Noah had a go at whittling a stick to a sharp point, the sort of thing Toby did. He made

some more paper darts for the blowpipes. They'd used up almost all the nails.

None of it was so much fun without Toby.

Where was he?

Perhaps Holly and he had gone to see their dad again, what with it being the summer holidays and that. Noah wished Toby had said.

When Zeke came to take over at the lookout, Noah went home, to find out from the computer how to make a proper pond.

It sounded expensive. You had to buy special pond liner stuff.

He would have to make do without that.

He flipped to the web pages about Sites of Special Scientific Interest, but there was too much writing. It gave him a headache.

Dad was working at the kitchen table: he made Noah a sandwich to take with him outside.

Noah fetched the spade from the greenhouse. It was too hot in there: he propped the door open to let in some air.

He took the spade with him down to the boggy patch near the bamboo at the bottom corner of the Wilderness.

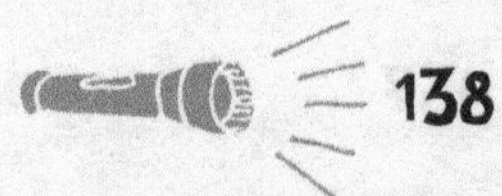

It made sense to dig the pond here, where the ground was already waterlogged. There must be an underground spring or stream or something, and if he dug a hole deep enough, and lined it stones, maybe it would be good enough for newts and frogs. Dragonflies might come too. That's what it had said on the computer. *Like magic, they arrive as if from thin air . . .*

Crow watched from the top of the pear tree.

Noah dug deep into the squishy ground. Water puddled up as he dug, filling the hole and swilling round in a muddy pool. It was very satisfying. He hunted for small flat rocks and stones to go on the bottom and then he had a better idea, and searched through the dump for something that might work as a pond lining. Finally under a smelly stinky pile of wet leaves and grass clippings he found a blue plastic sack. He cut it to the right size with the kitchen knife he'd left in the bramble den, big enough to cover the bottom and up the sides of the hole, and he weighted it back down with the flat pebbles. The water was muddy, but it would clear once the soil had settled down to the bottom. Perfect. Now he needed some plants to go round the edges, and pond-weed and water snails to keep the water clean—but from where?

Anil and Asha spilled out of their front door. They raced down the Wilderness to see what Noah was up to.

'It's brilliant!' Asha floated a bramble flower on the water and watched the pale pink petals spiral round on the surface.

'We need plants at the edge, for insects and creatures to hide in,' Noah said.

Asha dug up a clump of pink flowers with fine lacy leaves, and Noah replanted them at the edge of the pond. A small orange butterfly hovered over the water and rested for a second on one of the flowers.

'Wow!' Asha said. 'Beautiful.'

'Butterflies are solar-powered,' Noah said. 'They need the sun to make their wings work.'

'Like me!' Asha flapped her arms.

Anil moved in for a close-up of the butterfly. *Click. Click-click.* 'What is it? How rare?'

'A small Skipper,' Noah said. 'Not rare at all.'

A blue car reversed down the street. Toby and Holly's dad's car. So they HAD gone out earlier.

Noah stood up to wave. But Toby and Holly ran straight inside number seven, and the door banged shut behind

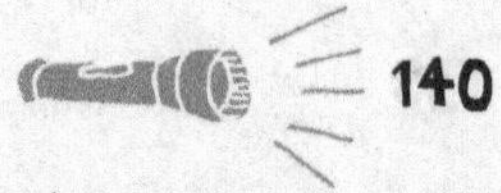

them. Their dad drove back up the street much too fast. The air stank of burned clutch.

Asha and Anil looked at each other, and then at Noah. 'What was all that about?' Anil said.

'Something's up,' Asha said. 'I'll ask Holly, later.'

'That bird is back.' Anil nodded towards Crow, perched on the pear tree.

'He's a crow,' Noah said. 'Corvid family. They are very intelligent. They can even work things out, like how to use tools.'

Anil laughed. 'Like, dig with a spade?'

'No, duh-brain. Things like, they deliberately drop nuts on the road so that the traffic will crush the hard shell and then they can eat the inside.'

'How is *that* using tools?'

'And they can work out things, like how to scoop up water using an old cup so they can have a drink. And other things.'

Anil hooted with laughter. 'You're kidding me.'

'Never mind him,' Asha said. 'It doesn't matter. Your crow is intelligent. It's following you, because it knows you have food.'

Noah put his hand in his pocket to find seed, but instead his hand closed round the small metal bell he'd put there earlier for safe-keeping. He'd forgotten all about it.

He pulled it out of his pocket and held it out for Asha. 'Look!'

'Oh!' She shook the bell, and its thin sound echoed over the Wilderness. She smiled. 'Thank you. Where did you find it?'

He hesitated. 'The new girl—Phoebe—she found it, in the grass.' He didn't tell Asha the rest. He didn't know why not.

Asha glanced up the street, and Noah looked too. There was no sign of the girl now.

'Maybe the little gold bowl . . .' She didn't finish her sentence.

Noah nodded. 'That might turn up, too.'

'So,' Anil said. 'How do we get newts to turn up? Can we buy some?'

'You have to wait,' Noah said. 'They find the pond, eventually, like the butterfly and dragonflies and the frogs and toads and other wild creatures. You have to be patient.'

'Only we can't,' Anil said. 'Realistically, Noah, we don't have time for that.'

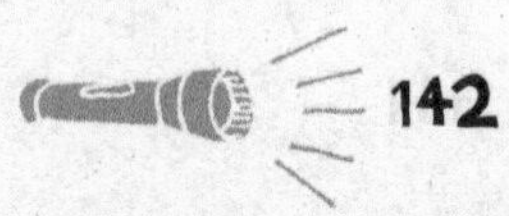

Noah turned away, so Anil couldn't see his face.

Asha knew he was upset. 'The tree man will be back—'

'—in only *two* days,' Noah said.

'—But there's more time before the council planning meeting happens. How long does a newt need?'

Noah didn't know.

There had to be newts nearby in the first place, for the pond plan to work.

And maybe there simply weren't any.

It was hopeless.

They'd have to stick with Toby's plans. Fight whoever came near.

Tree man. Council planners. Builders. The lot.

Wednesday 30th July

Chapter 18

Wednesday morning, Crow woke Noah up. The bird tapped on the skylight glass, and called in his croaky voice. *Craak, craak!*

Noah was on first watch. He ran straight to the lookout, checked everything was in place. Crow followed him and perched in the branch just above his head. It was nice, having company.

In his head, Noah went over the plan of what to do when the tree man turned up. It could easily be today.

1 Bang the drum really loud.

2 Every one run to their den-base. Take up weapons and ammo. Load spud guns and water pistols.

3 If tree man falls into trap, move position: everyone climb up the trees (not Natalie) with weapons, and make loud protest holding up photos of birds and nests. (Had Anil printed these off? Noah wasn't sure. He should check, later.)

4 If man somehow avoids man-traps and advances, vanguard team (Toby, Zeke, Holly) attack man with spud guns, water pistols etc while team B (Noah, Anil, Asha) climb up trees (see 3).

What next?

Toby had been a bit vague about the next part. Noah guessed they stayed up the trees until the man went away. So maybe they needed to bring food supplies, too?

What was that noise?

Half rumble, half engine-roar, accompanied by beeps.

Noah leapt up.

At the top of the street, a large vehicle was trying to reverse round the corner into their street. It sounded like the bin lorry, but it most definitely wasn't.

It was some sort of truck with a massive yellow digger strapped on top. Only the truck was too big to manoeuvre around the narrow corner.

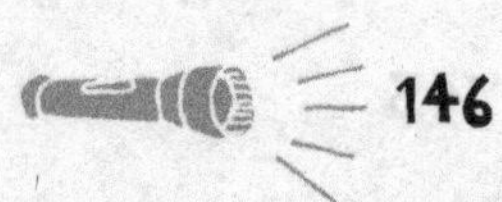

Two men jumped out of the cab. People were shouting—a traffic jam was forming on the top road.

Noah's brain struggled to make sense of what he was staring at.

Not the Tree Solutions man.

Something much worse.

An actual digger.

For a second, he panicked. Then he sprang into action. He banged the drums, one after the other, then both together, as loud as he could. The sound echoed out over the Wilderness. But it still didn't seem loud enough to carry as far as the houses.

Noah clambered down the tree; he jumped from too high up and twisted his ankle as he landed. He ran anyway, despite the pain, across the Wilderness to Toby's.

He hammered on Toby and Holly's door. This was a total emergency. There was no time to lose. He hammered more, and the door opened.

'Oh, it's you, Noah! Is everything all right?' Toby's mum was still in her dressing gown, her hair all mussed up.

'No. I need Toby. Holly. Everyone. Quick. There's a digger. It's an emergency!'

Toby was already halfway down the stairs, pulling on

his jeans and boots. Holly appeared at the top of the stairs. 'What's happened?'

'There's a digger on a lorry and it's coming down our street. Well, it's still at the top, but it will be here any second.' Noah was breathless with the horror of it.

'You run and get Zeke. We'll call Anil and Asha.'

Their mum stepped back as Toby pushed past. 'Would one of you explain exactly what's going on?'

But Toby was outside, pounding on the next door.

Noah belted up the street to Zeke's. Ouch. His ankle hurt.

Zeke was already at his door by the time Noah got there.

Zeke grabbed a spud gun and a sharp stick.

'Have you seen? They're bringing a digger in!'

'Good thing we made that man-trap at the very top,' Zeke said. 'A digger won't get very far.'

'But what if it goes round it?'

'The driver won't know it's there, so he won't know to go round it, will he?'

They both looked up the street. The lorry seemed to be wedged at the top. It hadn't got any closer.

'It's totally illegal and against the law,' Anil said, joining them.

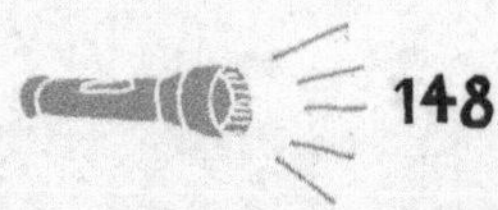

Asha and Holly rushed up the hill.

'Where's Toby?' Noah asked.

'Getting stuff.'

Someone needed to take charge. And Toby wasn't here!

Noah thought fast. There wasn't time for Toby's plan. They had to stop the digger getting anywhere near the Wilderness right this minute . . .

Noah took a deep breath. 'Everyone link arms. We'll make an actual human barrier.'

'Great! Like the suffragettes!' Holly put on her fierce face and stood square, arms out sideways. Asha stood next to her, arms wide, fingertips touching.

Impressive, Noah thought. He wouldn't want to mess with them!

The new girl was at the window, watching them.

'Let's get Phoebe to join us,' Holly said. 'The more the better.'

'No!' Noah said firmly.

'Why not? Don't be mean, Noah!'

'She's . . . she went in your den, Holly. And she pinches stuff.'

Asha stared. 'You mean . . . my little bell?'

Noah hesitated. Perhaps she *had* just found it in the grass . . . It was possible. He didn't have any proof.

'Never mind about all that now,' Holly said. 'This is much more important.'

'I'm going to check out exactly what's happening up there,' Anil said.

'No, come back! We need you here—' Noah said, but Anil was already running up the street.

This was all going wrong.

Phew! There was Toby at last, staggering up the street with a catapult and a bag of ammo and a huge water gun.

'Idiots! Why aren't you armed? Get your weapons FAST! Zeke, you take the pistol.'

Zeke fired a spurt of water at a lamp post. 'Cool!'

Asha and Holly ran to get their spud guns.

Toby set up the catapult with a stone from the bag. 'It takes skill,' he said. 'In the wrong hands, it can be lethal. A stone aimed at the head can kill a man.'

Holly rushed back up the road. 'Toby, I don't think that's a very good idea. We don't want to actually murder anyone.'

'I'll just scare them off. Show them we're totally serious.'

Anil jogged back down the hill. 'The lorry's stuck on the

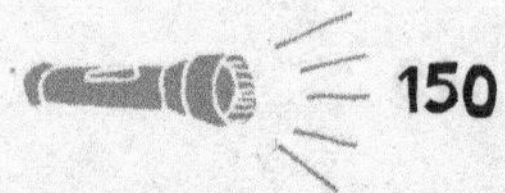

corner!' he puffed as he got closer. 'There's this huge traffic jam along the main road. Everyone's getting cross. The lorry driver called someone and they've got to tow the lorry away. So, there's no digger delivery today. BUT—' he paused, for maximum effect—'they'll be back tomorrow morning with a smaller lorry and a mini-digger.'

Toby exploded. He pulled back the catapult and aimed at the concrete kerb.

Peeee-owwww!

Everyone jumped back as the stone shattered like shrapnel.

'Stop it!' Holly said. 'You're not helping, being so angry. We need to *think*. Use our *brains*. Someone?'

'Well,' Noah said slowly. 'OK. We know it's a man and a digger we've got to fight, so . . .'

Toby butted in. 'We'll set up permanent camp on the Wilderness, and wage war exactly as we planned. Vanguard action—team A—to take out the digger man, followed by a second wave of attack by team B. We'll do another practice.'

'Why not Noah's human chain?' Asha tried to ask, but she was drowned out by Toby firing the catapult again. This time, the stone hit the road.

'We should put up really big protest signs, with "Save The Land" and stuff like that,' Holly said, 'so everyone can see the message we want to get across.'

'The whole digger thing is still illegal,' Anil said. 'Totally undemocratic.'

'We haven't had letters. No one's got planning permission,' Asha said.

'That's all irrelevant now,' Toby said. 'We're fighting a *war*.'

Toby fired another volley of shot.

'Stop it!' Holly shouted. 'Calm down!'

Noah watched Nat walk slowly up the hill from number fifteen, her newly-plastered arm in a clean white sling.

'Mum's cross with you, Noah,' she called in a sing-song voice, soon as she got close enough. With her good arm, she waved at Phoebe, watching from the window at number thirty.

'Shut *up*,' Noah said. 'Go away.'

Nat turned her back on him, and wandered across the road. The door at number thirty opened. Phoebe stood in the open doorway.

They all watched as Nat kept walking, straight inside. The door shut behind her.

'*Whaat*?'

'Leave her be, Noah,' Holly said. 'Concentrate. So. What else do we need?'

'Tents,' Zeke said. 'I saw it on telly. Tents, and tunnels. Concrete ones, underground. You chain yourself to things, so no one can move you off.'

'That's ridiculous. We're trying to stop people putting concrete down!'

'It was on the news. You don't wash your hair ever and you wear really dirty clothes and cook beans on a fire. And play music in hammocks in the trees. It's awesome.'

'We don't need tents. We can sleep in our dens,' Asha said.

'Not all night, really,' Holly said. 'Ours doesn't have a roof.'

'Mine neither.' Noah was still angry with Nat. What was she playing at?

'We should get more weapons ready, to sabotage any vehicles trying to get on site.' Zeke aimed the water gun in Toby's direction.

Toby loaded another stone in his catapult, ready to fire back.

Holly stepped forward. 'Stop it, you two. *Please*? Let's just focus. Noah, what do you think?'

'I think, it would be good to have one big tent for all of us to sleep in together, tonight, so we are all together and ready for the morning. The battle stations are weapons bases and hide-outs for the daytime attack, not for sleeping in.'

'OK. So who has a big tent? Zeke?'

'No.'

'We don't either,' Noah said.

Asha shook her head. 'No.'

Holly and Toby looked at each other. There was a long silence.

'Our dad does,' Toby finally mumbled. 'Massive one.'

'Great. Can you get it?' Noah said.

Toby shrugged. He turned his back to them, as if he didn't want them to see his face.

'It's a bit complicated,' Holly said. 'But Toby can try.'

'Dani might have a festival pop-up one,' Zeke said. 'I'll ask her. But it'll be tiny.'

'OK,' Holly said. 'So. Everyone get prepared. Tell parents it's a sleepover. Nothing else. Simples. Toby will get the tent off Dad. Everyone make official protest signs – "Keep Off our Wilderness" sort of thing. We can use that yellow paint we found. Bring sleeping bags and food and we'll make a fire. Agreed?'

'Yes!'

'And make sure all your weapons are ready. Don't waste any more ammo.'

'Get back up the lookout, Noah,' Toby said. 'There might be other invaders, for all we know.'

Phoebe's front door opened. Nat grinned at them.

Noah stared.

Natalie called Asha and Holly over.

'Not *you*, Noah. It's just for *girls*.' She smirked.

Just girls?

He didn't want to go inside Phoebe's house with them, of course not, but it still felt mean and horrible, being excluded.

Luckily Holly and Asha saw sense. 'We can't play with you now, Nat. Sorry, we're really busy,' Holly said.

They had less than twenty-four hours to get totally ready for the Wilderness War.

Chapter 19

Noah kept watch. A few cars came down the street. Each time he heard an engine, his heart raced.

The door opened at his own house. Mum.

Noah groaned. He watched her come up the path in her bright turquoise sundress and flip-flops. Where was she going? Not work. To the shops, most likely. She had a bag over her shoulder.

Noah willed her to keep going up the road, straight past. But of course she didn't.

Mum crossed over the road. 'Noah?' she called. 'Natalie!'

She still hadn't spotted him. He clambered down fast and walked up the Wilderness.

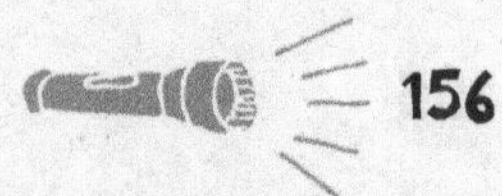

She frowned. 'Where's Natalie?'

'In there.' He pointed up to number thirty. 'With the new girl, Phoebe.'

'OK.' Mum nodded. 'So, Noah, what was all that noise and kerfuffle about, so very early this morning? So urgent and important that you haven't had any breakfast, or said good morning to your family.'

Noah shuffled away from Toby and Zeke's dens, closer to the road and to Mum. Even so, he knew they'd be listening.

'Sorry,' Noah said. That was the best way to start, with Mum. 'But there was a lorry coming down the road, and I got worried about the Wilderness trees again, so I went to get the others. It was an emergency. But it turned out to be a false alarm.' Best to tell the truth that far.

Mum nodded again. 'So, what are you up to now?'

'Just mucking about. Planning a sleepover, tonight, outside. If that's OK? Please, Mum? Everyone else's mum has said yes.' That was a small white lie so he crossed his fingers behind his back so it wouldn't count.

'A sleepover out here, with all your friends from the street?' Mum narrowed her eyes, examining his face.

'Yes. And Toby's dad's got a big tent we can all share. And

we can make a tiny safe fire, to cook some dough on. If you say yes. Please.'

Mum nodded. 'OK. It sounds fun. But Natalie's too little. So be nice to her, she'll be upset she can't join in.'

Noah nodded.

'I'll get some food for you all. Marshmallows, perhaps? To toast over a small campfire, very carefully, like we used to do with Nana and Grandpa.'

'Yes! Thanks, Mum!'

'Best make the most of this place, while you still can.'

Her words rang in his ears, long after she'd gone up the road and disappeared round the corner.

Mum thought the Wilderness would soon be gone. That was why she was being nice about the sleepover. Why she'd stopped being cross with him so quickly.

Zeke's head appeared. 'Nice one!' he said. 'Well played.'

Toby popped up too, out of his den.

'You have to get that tent off your dad, Toby,' Noah said. 'Or we're stuffed.'

*

Noah saw Toby traipse up the hill by himself, off to see his dad to get the tent. He didn't actually say where he was

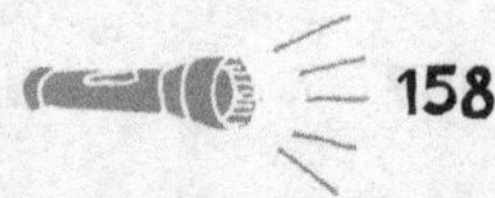

going, but Noah guessed. He'd got clean clothes on, and had smoothed down his hair.

Anil was on watch.

A kind of stillness had fallen over everything. It was as if everything was waiting, holding its breath. The tarmac on the road shimmered, baked by the sun. The birds were quiet in the heat; only the grasshoppers chirred and chirruped.

Noah waded through the long grass to check the pond.

The water had cleared since yesterday.

He crouched down to see better.

Amazing. Just like it said on the website, things had arrived at the pond overnight. How did that happen? Tiny water snails moved very, very slowly across the pebbles at the bottom. A small bug scooted across the water as if by magic—really, Noah knew, it was paddling along the surface with its oar-like hind legs.

He lay down on his front, to get a closer look. Yes, it was a water boatman. Water bugs were usually first to arrive at a new pond, then other flying things like dragonflies, then the frogs and newts and other species that might already be lurking in damp spots in the Wilderness might turn up. Given time.

Except, time had almost run out.

There were only hours left, now.

Crow swooped low and landed with a bit of a tumble beside the pond.

'Not very graceful,' Noah said. He couldn't help laughing.

Crow didn't like that. He strutted off, ignoring Noah even when he pulled a handful of seeds from his pocket.

'Suit yourself, moody.' Noah crawled forward so he was leaning out over the pond. Up really close, a water boatman was fascinating. He tried to spot the bubble of air. He needed a magnifying glass, really.

Crow sidled up. He perched himself at the edge of the pond.

For a second Noah thought Crow was going to gobble up the bug, but Crow wanted a drink, that's all. He took one beakful at a time: in between, he looked all around, keeping a beady eye out for danger.

Noah moved away from the edge of the pond and turned onto his back. He lay on the hot grass, crushing it beneath him to make a sort of shallow nest, with the tall grass and weeds all around, hiding him from the world. A bee buzzed over the fine umbrellas of white flowers. The grasshoppers whirred and clicked.

If only he could simply lie like this in the sunny Wilderness watching the insects come to the pond, and the birds, and the clouds whizzing across the sky, and drift in his own thoughts. That's what summer holidays used to be like, with no school or anything else to worry about.

Not this summer.

He imagined the digger arriving in the morning, the caterpillar tracks running over and squashing everything in their way, and the wide metal jaws of the yellow digger grabbing and chewing and spitting out all the wild flowers and weeds and earth that were home to the insects and creatures he loved.

It was harder to imagine actually *stopping* it.

For a second, he wished he could be like Toby. Toby was confident they'd do it. Toby was actually looking forward to fighting.

'Hey, Noah!' Holly called.

He sat up.

Holly, Asha, Nat, and Phoebe were skipping down the street together. They were each carrying things—posts? flagpoles?—no, banners, and big signs in bright colours stuck on wooden sticks.

'Look what we've made!' Holly and Asha held up either end of a big banner made of white sheet, with bright yellow letters spelling . . .

SAVE OUR WILDERNESS!!!

'And mine!' Nat said. Her banner was covered with sparkly stuff—flowers and butterflies:

Noah read Phoebe's sign. It was rather long, but not bad, considering.

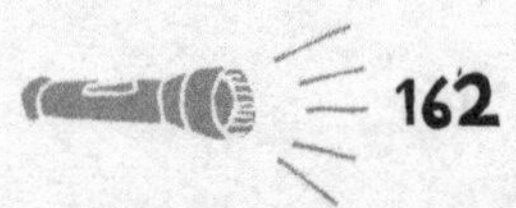

SAVE THE WILDERNESS:
HOMES FOR BIRDS AND
BUTTERFLIES AND BEES AND BATS,
AND SNAKES AND STUFF, NOT
HORRIBLE HOUSES FOR HUMANS.

Phoebe was good at handwriting. She could write really big, neat letters and somehow space it all out right, so the words fit on the cardboard.

Whenever Noah tried to do something like a sign or a poster at school, it always went wrong. His letters would get smaller as they went along the line, or he'd run out of space and have to do a hyphen in the middle of a word like WILDER – NESS, and it ended up looking really stupid.

'Well?' Holly said. 'What do you think, Noah? Aren't we all amazing?'

'Err . . . yes,' Noah said. 'Yes, really good.'

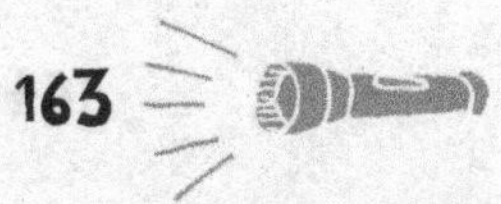

'We had such a lovely time,' Nat said. 'Phoebe's got a whole huge box of amazing pens and glitter and stickers.'

Phoebe smiled for the first time.

Noah sighed. That was all he needed: Nat and Phoebe, best friends. She'd be in his house next, and going through his stuff. What did she know about bees and butterflies, in any case? Did she even care? It was all put on.

And there weren't any snakes.

'You need to get your sleeping bags and food ready for tonight.'

Nat's face lit up with excitement.

Noah didn't tell her what Mum had said, about being too young. Not allowed. He'd let Mum deal with the fall-out.

'Where shall we put our signs?' Nat said.

'In the dens, ready for the morning,' Holly said.

'What time's it all happening?' Phoebe asked, as if it was a party or something.

'Eight-thirty, nine, maybe,' Holly said. 'But we'll be up much earlier.'

'Phoebe isn't allowed to sleep out with us,' Holly said quickly, as if she'd guessed what Noah was thinking.

'What have you been doing?' she asked him.

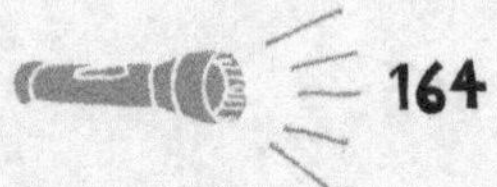

'Lookout duty, and me and Toby made some more arrow flights with feathers. Then he went off.'

'To get the tent?'

Noah nodded.

'Good.'

Phoebe and Nat climbed into the pirate den.

'Any newts yet?' Holly asked.

'No.'

Holly looked a bit weird, Noah thought. She was watching Phoebe trying out the ropes for the sail, laughing with Natalie.

'Where's Asha?' Noah asked.

'Looking up stuff on the computer. Laws and that.' She turned back to Noah. 'So, we'll get our camping things ready and come back here, yes?'

'I'll go and make the dough, to cook on the fire,' Noah said. 'Call me if you need me.'

Chapter 20

Toby still wasn't back.

It was evening, and the Wilderness was deep in shadow.

They'd have to improvise, Holly said, until Toby arrived with the tent, at which point they could all move their stuff into it. But they couldn't hang about any longer. It was better to get on and use their dens for now.

Anil and Asha put candles in jam jars to make a path of flickering light down the slope to their den. They arranged sleeping bags and pillows inside and hung up a lantern.

Holly carried cushions and blankets down to the pirate ship to make a bed.

Zeke pitched his sister Dani's pop-up tent on the long grass near one of the man-traps, and shoved her old sleeping bag inside, ready for later.

'Careful you don't step on your own traps in the dark!' Asha said.

Everyone laughed, imagining it.

Noah had left Natalie behind, crying and carrying on in her bedroom, because Mum and Dad said she couldn't join in.

There was no sign of Phoebe, thank goodness.

And where was Toby? Why was he taking so long?

'How far is it?' Noah asked.

'Not far in the car. But he'd have to get a bus there. What if he got lost?'

'Nah,' Noah said. 'He'd have a compass and map and everything, even on a bus. You know Tobes.'

Holly's voice went quieter. 'Sometimes Mum worries about Toby never talking about things, like feelings. He misses Dad all the time.'

Noah didn't know what to say to that.

'Let's get the fire going,' he said instead. 'I'll show you how to cook dough on sticks.'

Noah was already picking up bits of dry wood for kindling.

He chose a good place for the fire, away from the trees and the fence, like Grandpa had taught him. He cleared away all the grass in the middle, down to the bare earth, and put stones around the edge, so the fire couldn't spread and catch light to anything.

Everyone helped. They dragged old logs over to make seats around the fire.

'Matches, anyone?' Noah asked. Toby would've used his special flint striker to light a bundle of dry moss and bark to start the fire.

Zeke rummaged in his pockets and produced a box. It felt like cheating, Noah thought, but Toby wasn't here.

Zeke struck the match.

Orange flames licked along the edge of scrunched-up paper. The dry grass and bark caught alight, and the fire began to crackle. Smoke spiralled up as the twigs began to burn. Noah added bigger bits of wood. Some of it was still damp, and steamed instead of burning properly. He pulled those bits away, and found a dry plank which burned bright and hot. Sparks danced up into the cool air. Everyone settled closer to the warmth of the fire. The smoke went straight up: there was no wind tonight.

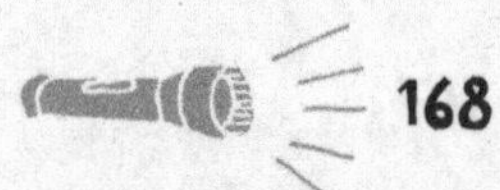

'Wow,' Zeke said. 'It's awesome. Our own fire.'

'It's as if the firelight holds back the dark,' Asha said. 'It makes it feel safe.'

'It is safe!' Anil said.

'Not for much longer,' Noah said. 'Nothing's safe any more. This might be the very last time *ever* we have a fire and stay out on the Wilderness all night.'

Holly nodded. 'I know. It's scary.'

'Everything hangs on what happens tomorrow,' Zeke said.

'It's up to us,' Noah said. 'We have to fight for the Wilderness. For all the plants and creatures and trees. They can't fight for themselves.'

'Exactly,' Holly said.

No one said anything for a long time. They were all thinking about Noah's words. They sat close together and watched the fire.

It died down to white-hot embers, perfect for cooking.

Noah picked up his bag and fished out a plastic box. 'I've made flour and water dough, to cook on sticks,' he said. 'You get a twig and peel the bark so it's clean, then you dip it in the flour mixture and twirl it like this . . . so it stays on while you cook it over the fire.'

For a while everyone was busy, toasting dough sticks and eating the hot bread.

'Whoops!' Anil dropped his stick into the fire by mistake. He tried again with a longer stick.

'Marshmallows, next.' Noah produced a packet from his bag.

There was an art to toasting these, too. If you left the stick over the fire too long the marshmallow turned to a brittle toffee or slid off into the fire in a gooey mess.

'Sooo deliciously sweet and yummy!' Asha licked her fingers and threaded another pink sugary marshmallow onto a stick.

Holly stood up as a car reversed down the hill.

'Toby?' Noah asked.

She nodded. 'Dad's car, anyway.' She was already running.

They watched her go. It was hard to see what was happening, in the dark.

Noah put another log on the fire. No one said anything. Even the background roar of traffic died down. The fire hissed and spat and sizzled.

An owl hooted from one of the tall trees. Another one answered it.

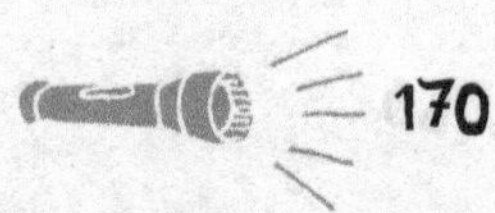

'Tawny owls,' Noah said. 'I wish I could actually *see* them. But I never do.'

'I'm still hungry,' Zeke said. 'Anyone got more food?'

Anil rummaged in a bag. He laid out two packets of biscuits, some cheese triangles, and a tub of mini flapjacks. 'Help yourself.'

Asha shivered. 'I wish they'd hurry up. Holly went up ages ago. My back's cold.'

'Turn round, then. Warm your back up.'

'What's that?' Zeke said.

'Someone's coming!'

Toby and Holly loomed out of the darkness. Between them, they carried a huge canvas bag.

'Ta-dah!' Holly said. 'Behold at last the wondrous tent!'

Chapter 21

None of them had put up a big tent in the dark before by themselves. Toby pretended he knew how, but he obviously didn't.

'Aren't there instructions?' Anil asked.

'No. It was second-hand,' Holly said. 'Dad bought it for going on holiday in France . . . only, we never went.'

'So, you've never put it up before? Maybe there's a bit missing?'

'There is not,' Holly snapped. 'And we did put it up once, in Cornwall.'

Toby wrestled with the flapping canvas, trying to get it over the metal frame. He couldn't reach.

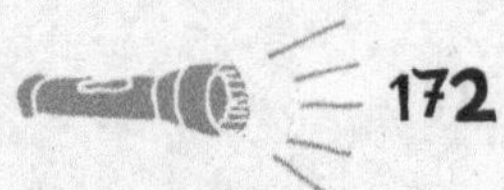

Noah felt useless. He hadn't a clue.

'I remember!' Toby suddenly said. 'You do it with the frame halfway up first and then you put the poles all the way up.'

It began to look more like an actual tent. It was old, and heavy, made of orange canvas. Once it was up, they pegged out the guy ropes. It loomed up, massive in the dark.

Holly, Anil, Asha, and Zeke charged off to get their things from the dens.

'They're still acting like this is just for fun,' Noah said to Toby. 'It's as if they don't want to think about what's really happening in the morning.'

Noah looked at Toby. He seemed a bit quiet. 'Tent's great, Tobes,' he said. 'Thanks for getting it. Your dad OK?'

'He went off on one of his rants. About the land being sold, and planning permission and the council. I shouldn't have told him. Sorry.'

'It's OK. Everyone will know, after tomorrow.'

'Says he's going down the council offices. He'll just make things worse.'

'Might not. Might help,' Noah said.

'You don't know my dad.'

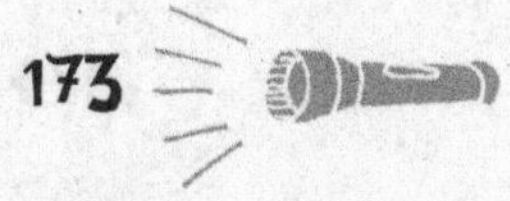

'Yes I do,' Noah said. 'Course I do.'

'Well, not the new version of Dad.'

'What do you mean?'

'The dad living in a horrid flat all by himself.'

There was nothing Noah could say about that.

Holly arrived with her pile of cushions and blankets. She spread them out inside the tent. They made one big bed in the end, and everyone crawled in together, exhausted.

'We'll go over the plan one more time,' Toby said.

Noah crawled over to lie at the open end of the tent, with the flaps tied back so he could see the sky. The stars were out. If he lay at the right angle, he couldn't see any houses or streetlights.

Everyone stopped talking. One by one, they fell asleep.

Noah gazed up at the chunk of moon and the canopy of stars.

Toby lay on his back too, staring up into the dark.

'You still awake?' Noah whispered, even though he knew he was.

'Yes.'

'Let's go back outside.'

'OK.'

Toby got the fire going again, blowing on the glowing embers and feeding the first small flame with dry bark and grass. The wind had got up; smoke blew back in their faces, but Noah liked the smell. It reminded him of bonfire night, and barbecues on the beach. Things he loved.

'We need to be mentally ready for tomorrow,' Toby said. 'Be in a totally positive mindset.'

'Do you want to go over the plan again?' Noah said.

'It'll be OK, as long as people do what they're supposed to. But things can change mid-battle. A good commander has to think on his feet. Change plans, if conditions change.'

Noah's chest hurt. The war was so close now.

He tried to think positive, like Toby said.

It was good to be sitting next to Toby in the dark like this, getting ready to defend their land. It was like being a cave-man, or an Iron Age man or something. It felt real.

If he moved away from the crackle of the fire he could hear a whole load more rustlings and squeaks and tiny sounds as insects and other creatures moved through the grass. Pale moths danced dangerously near the fire, drawn by the light.

There are hundreds and hundreds of different kinds of moths, Noah thought. And most people have absolutely no idea.

A late train rattled along the valley out of the city. A cat ran along the top of the fence and stopped to look at them with startled eyes. If only a fox would come, Noah thought. Or the deer. He'd give anything to see the deer tonight.

Perhaps if he slept now, and got up really early, he might have a chance of seeing it again. One *last* chance, if things went wrong tomorrow.

His eyes hurt from straining to see in the dark.

'Sleep?' he said to Toby.

Toby nodded. 'Best get some. We'll need energy for the fight.'

They crawled back into the tent.

Thursday 31st July

Chapter 22

The birdsong was deafening. It was dawn, the first light filtering through the trees. Noah rolled over so he could see out of the tent flaps. They'd left them open all night. The sky was a pearly grey.

No one else was awake.

His clothes still smelled of bonfire. He'd gone to sleep fully dressed. He crawled outside.

Toby muttered something in his sleep, but none of the others even stirred.

Crow flew down from the ash tree soon as he saw Noah. The other crows were making a racket, arguing over the nest. Noah ran to the greenhouse to get some more seed for

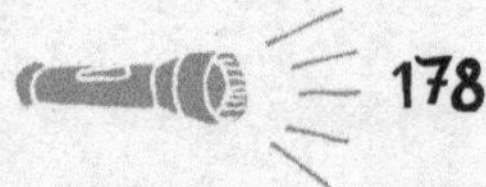

Crow's breakfast. The grass was sopping wet. Dew, not rain.

Crow knew the routine. He flew straight to the roof of the greenhouse and waited. He pecked straight out of Noah's hand without any fuss today. He flew back up to the tall tree to join in the argument with his crow family.

Noah sat in a patch of sunlight on the dry greenhouse floor with the door wide open. The Wilderness was alive with birds. He knew the names of some of them – crows and magpies, blackbirds, song thrushes, a robin, sparrows and chaffinches – but there were lots he didn't know. They flew from bush to bush, over the bramble den, between the pear tree and the ash trees. A large bumblebee droned from one flower to the next on the brambles; a tortoiseshell butterfly opened its wings out, taking in the early warmth of the sun.

Gradually the sun warmed Noah too. It must be about five-thirty, he reckoned. So he had maybe three precious hours, before the lorry arrived with the digger and the fight began in earnest.

Something moved the other side of the bramble patch.

Please, he wished over and over.

Please let it be the deer . . .

He watched and waited, keeping as still as he could, half-hidden in the greenhouse.

A whole family of magpies screeched across the grass: five all together, and then two more, he counted, that landed in the pear tree.

Seven for a secret . . .

It was a good sign. A kind of promise, he told himself.

And maybe he was right, because now he could definitely smell something—that musky, mysterious animal scent he'd smelled before. And the *something* moved again—he heard its feet, and the rustle of grass, and there . . .

Yes, there it was.

His deer. Its breath made misty clouds on the cool morning air. It was grazing, scraping at the ground with its front hoof, searching for something, eating, moving on. It lifted its head for a second, and Noah saw its dark eyes, and the small stubby horns on its head, and the dark nose, twitching, sniffing the air, alert and wary.

It must have smelled him. Noah was sure he hadn't moved, but the deer turned, and suddenly ran, its feet thudding over the grass. Noah ran after it, to see which way it

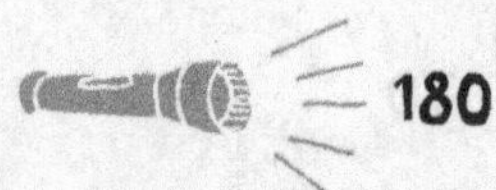

went. He ducked under the low branches of the shrubs, the rowan tree, the ash saplings next to the fence at the bottom of the Wilderness, and caught a final glimpse, as the deer pushed through a narrow gap in the fence and disappeared from view.

Noah peered through the gap. It led to the bottom of someone's garden, one of the modern houses in the road below. There were shrubs and fruit trees—a pear, like the one in the Wilderness, all crooked and gnarled with age. There was no sign of the deer now.

Noah grinned to himself. He felt like singing, or dancing, or something. There weren't any words, for what he felt like inside.

Chapter 23

Noah heard voices coming from the tent, and laughter. Toby hung his head out of the tent as Noah got closer. 'Where've you been?'

'I saw the deer,' Noah said. 'That's three times, now.'

'Why didn't you call me?'

'I would've, but it ran off. Sorry, Tobes.'

Toby nodded. 'Wow. That's amazing. I didn't believe you, before.'

'I know.'

'Most people wouldn't.' Toby thought for a second. 'You should get a photo of it.'

'It's not rare or anything,' Noah said. 'Just—' He didn't

know how to explain to Toby what it was like, seeing the deer.

Toby rummaged through various bags in the tent. 'Soggy flapjacks, two manky apples and a bruised banana for breakfast.'

'I'll go and raid our kitchen.'

Holly peered out of the tent, her hair all sticking up funny. 'See if Nat's awake. She can have breakfast with us.'

The front door was still on the latch, the way he'd left it last night. Mum would have made sure it was open all night in case he needed to come home for any reason. No one was up yet. Noah found cheese and milk in the fridge; he grabbed bowls off the kitchen shelves, took a bag of sliced bread and Nat's packet of Frosty-flakes out of the cupboard and shoved it all in a large carrier bag.

He lugged it outside.

Mr Moss was at his gate, watching the early morning sky.

'Morning, Noah! See our friend's still around.' Mr Moss nodded towards Crow, perched on the greenhouse.

'Yes, he's really tame now. He'll take the seed from my hand. He likes fruit too, and biscuits.'

'They'll eat almost anything, crows will. Omnivorous.'

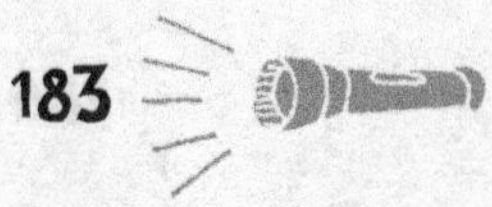

'And they're really intelligent. I read about it.'

'In one of them books I gave you?'

'On the computer,' Noah said.

'Ahh,' Mr Moss said. 'Well, that's how it is these days.' He looked closely at Noah. 'So what's all this carrying-on? You kids is up to something!'

Mr Moss wasn't like the other adults. He was . . . well, more like Noah, really. Only very, very old. Noah had a sudden urge to tell him what was happening.

The For Sale notice, the Tree Solutions man, the nests, the Wildlife and Countryside Act, the digger about to arrive: it all spilled out of him.

Mr Moss listened. He nodded and tutted. 'Years ago, I grew tomatoes and dahlias and all sorts on that precious patch of ground. All for a few pounds and shillings a year. And I still love to see all the birds and all the wild creatures. This a very sorry state of affairs.' His face creased up with sadness.

'But we're going to stop it happening,' Noah said quickly. 'We're all prepared. We've dug massive man-traps and made protest signs and everything.'

'Good lad,' Mr Moss said. 'I'd be with you on the front

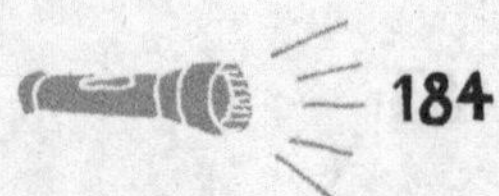

line, if it weren't for me gammy leg. I'll be there with you in spirit.' He raised his fist. 'Solidarity, comrade!'

Noah carried on down the hill to the tent.

'Cheese on toast, if we can get the fire going again,' Noah announced. 'Plus cereal. Even bowls and milk.'

'Spoons?' Holly asked.

'Who needs spoons?' Noah said.

'And did you tell Nat?'

'Oops. I forgot.'

'Duh!'

'Everyone up!' Toby shouted into the tent. 'We have to get ourselves into position soon.

'OK, boss.' Zeke buried his head under a cushion and fake-snored loudly, just to wind up Toby.

It worked.

Toby dragged Zeke out by his collar, yelling at him.

Holly shouted at Toby to calm down.

Zeke laughed so much he couldn't walk straight.

Noah gathered up dry bits of wood and remade the fire. Asha helped him. They used Toby's knife to cut cheese into slabs and piled it onto slices of bread. You had to balance it all perfectly on a stick and take it off the moment the cheese began to melt and bubble or it dribbled off and the bread burned.

Noah wasn't so hungry any more. His belly was too full of worry.

Toby patrolled up and down, buzzing with adrenaline, hurrying them up.

'Everyone needs to get into position by 07.45, armed and ready. Re-fill that water pistol, Zeke. You've wasted most of the water.'

'Why are you talking funny?' Zeke mimicked Toby. '*Oh-seven-forty-five*. What's all that about?'

'War talk,' Toby said. 'Get used to it.'

'Yes, Zeke.' Anil joined in. 'Man up. Remember what's at stake. All of this, lost forever. Imagine summers without the Wilderness. Imagine being stuck inside our houses all day, or having to go to a pathetic park; or a plastic *indoor play centre*.' He made a gagging sound.

'I know, I know.'

'Holly's back with Nat. Hey, Nat!' Asha paused. 'Oh. And Phoebe.'

Today she was wearing a pink sparkly top and white trousers.

'Phoebe's come to help,' Nat announced.

Noah groaned. But there was nothing he could do. And maybe there was a kind of safety in numbers.

'So,' Nat explained to Phoebe, 'that's my brother Noah, worst luck, and Toby is Holly's brother, and that's Zeke, and Anil. You've met Asha already.'

'Twins!' Phoebe said, as if she was a genius, working it out for herself.

She wanted to see inside the tent. She trampled all over the sleeping-bags-bed and bounced on the cushions. 'Cool!' She kept saying. 'A-maz-ing!'

Toby spoke to Phoebe. 'Did Holly explain? You have to do what I say. I'm in charge.'

Phoebe's lip moved ever so slightly, but she didn't say anything. She stopped bouncing.

For a second Noah wondered if she was going to laugh. He still didn't trust her.

Her white trousers were already stained with grass and mud, but she didn't seem to mind. She asked a billion questions about everything. What were their names again? Which were their houses? How long had they live there? How come they all knew each other? Where did they go to school? Why not the same school? What were they doing? Why? How come they were allowed to play out by themselves? Wasn't it dangerous to sleep in a tent like that? How come they were allowed knives and catapults and stuff? What was it like being a twin? What country were they from? ('England!' Asha said, rolling her eyes at Anil.)

'I'm going up the lookout,' Noah told Toby. 'In case the digger comes early.'

'Good.'

'Today's the 31st,' Noah said. 'What if the tree man turns up too, with the chainsaw?'

'Same drill,' Toby said. 'We can handle it. Two for the price of one!'

Toby called everyone else over.

'OK, it's time to go. Set up the banners and stuff first. Smear your faces with mud for camouflage. Then man the dens. Prepare weapons. Hide. No one speak or move until I give the signal. We have to surprise the man. Vanguard A, ready for first attack, once he's started moving onto the land. If necessary, use pincer strategy to steer him towards the traps. Team B move into attack in the second wave, so Team A can refuel ammo. Listen out for the drum.'

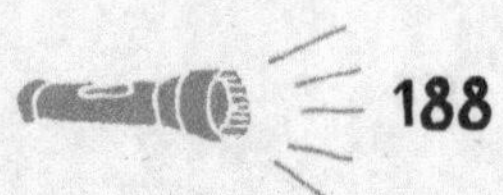

Phoebe giggled.

Toby glared at her. 'It's not a game,' he said. 'This is for real.'

He led the way up the hill.

Noah watched from the lookout. The girls chattered together as if they were already best friends with Phoebe. Even Asha seemed to like her now. They tied the biggest banner between two trees at the top of the Wilderness, and planted the other signs along the kerb edge.

High in his tree, Noah picked up the bow and checked the supply of arrows. He made sure the water bucket was balanced right. He picked up his stick, ready to strike the paint can.

They were ready.

Chapter 24

The lorry rumbled along the main road. The sound got louder as it came closer, closer. The lorry slowed down as it reached the turning for Pear Tree Buildings and prepared to reverse.

This was it.

Noah banged the drum, over and over, a loud, rhythmic beat that got faster and faster, like his own racing heart.

Beep. Beep. Beep . . . A truck with a bright orange mini-digger strapped on top edged very slowly round the corner into Pear Tree Buildings and reversed down the hill. It braked outside number thirty-two and parked.

Noah felt totally sick.

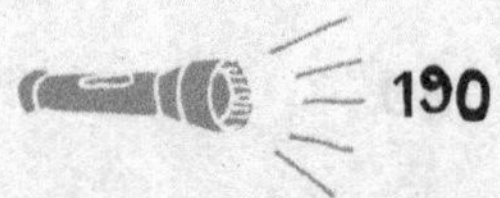

He crouched down, so he was hidden in the canopy of leaves.

He heard Toby shuffling about in his den, getting ready to attack. Out of the corner of his eye he glimpsed Phoebe standing up in the pirate ship and someone—Holly—grabbing her back down.

The cab door swung open and a man jumped down.

The man scratched his head. He climbed back into the cab. He settled back in his seat.

What was he doing?

He must have seen the banners. And the tent: in the sunlight, it glowed like a massive beacon.

The man switched on the cab radio.

Noah heard a tinny pop song, then some talking and a traffic update. The radio must be turned up really loud.

The man looked at his phone and tapped his fingers on the dashboard in time with the music. He unwrapped a sandwich and ate it. It was as if he was deliberately taking his time.

Did he suspect something?

Eventually, he opened the cab door again, and pressed some kind of lever to lower the back of the truck. He checked something back inside the cab—the handbrake, perhaps,

Noah thought. This hill was a bit steep if you weren't used to it. He thought of Toby and the go-kart that time . . .

If the lorry handbrake wasn't on properly, and the engine not in gear, the lorry might start to roll down the hill . . .

In his mind's eye, Noah saw truck-plus-digger hurtling down the hill, gathering speed, taking out the parked cars in its way . . . landing with a huge almighty deafening CRASH at the bottom, narrowly missing the line of garages in the street below. Or not. Bursting into flames, a massive fireball destroying the entire neighbourhood . . .

Now the man walked slowly round to the back of the truck. He climbed up the ramp and untied the straps on the digger. He whistled as he worked.

Something pinged through the air and hit the cab with a loud clunk. A stone, from Toby's catapult.

The man stopped, looked around. He examined the stone. He walked round the truck to check the other side. He scratched his head.

Good shot. Hold your nerve, Toby. Noah breathed out.

The man went back to untie the rest of the straps.

Wait, Noah willed the others. He knew Zeke would be desperate to pile in.

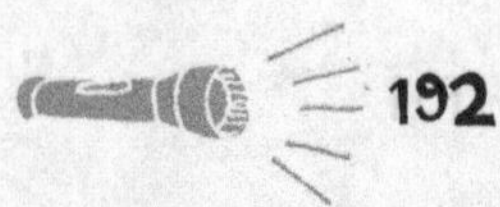

This was good, so far. The man had seen the banners, but he had absolutely no idea they were all lying in wait ready to attack.

The man sat down on the seat of the mini-digger and started the engine. He carefully drove the digger down the ramp, onto the road. It tipped at an alarming angle. He parked it so it was wedged against the kerb, engine running, got off, and strolled across the road as if he was the only person for miles.

He stared across the Wilderness. He looked at the big tent and frowned.

Noah saw the door on Toby's den shift slightly.

Toby's head emerged, his face streaked with mud. Then one hand, holding the catapult. He glanced up, and nodded at Noah.

Further over, Zeke's head appeared from his den, too. He was watching for Toby to give the signal.

The man walked back to the mini-digger, fastened his yellow safety helmet, climbed in, and revved the engine.

The digger crawled on its caterpillar tracks across the road towards the edge of the Wilderness. The angle of the hill, combined with the camber of the road, made it difficult to steer straight.

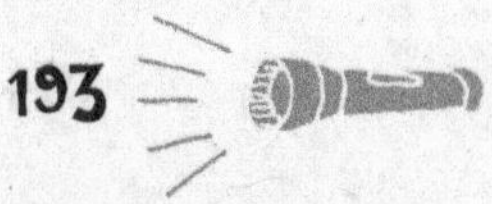

So far, so good.

If the man kept going in that direction, he'd drive straight onto the camouflaged man-trap and fall in. But was it big and deep enough, Noah wondered, to derail the digger?

'Go! Go !Go!' Toby yelled as he and Zeke went over the top, firing as they went.

A spurt of water caught the man in the face. He let out an angry roar.

Holly and Phoebe rushed up the hill, spud guns loaded.

Potato pellets showered the back of the man's neck as he tried to dry his face on his grubby T-shirt. He yelled out. 'Oi! You hooligans! What the heck are you playing at?'

Still Toby yelled, a rallying war cry.

Noah clambered down the tree. Anil joined him. They crept across the Wilderness, shooting arrows and firing with blowpipes. None of them actually hit the man, but the flurry of arrows and potato and water and now, a rain of darts from Zeke's blowpipe, turned the man's rage up another notch.

He rammed the digger into gear and lurched forward, as if he meant to run them all down. 'I don't believe it! Nutters! Get out of the way! Someone will get *hurt*!'

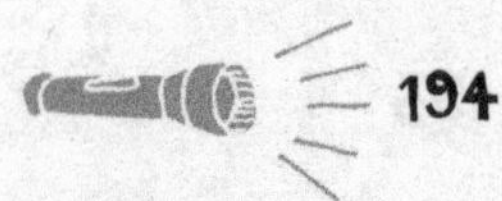

'You!' Toby shouted. '*Get off our land!*'

Toby began to chant.

'*Keep off. Keep off!*'

'Keep off! No diggers!' everyone yelled. They waved the banners and signs.

Phoebe had the loudest voice. She shouted the words like a pro.

Toby changed the chant. 'What do we want?'

'*Our land!*' Holly yelled back.

'When do we want it?'

'*Now!*'

Natalie was shaking. 'It's OK,' Noah whispered to her. 'There's seven of us. Against one of him.'

'Eight,' Holly said, 'counting Phoebe.'

The engine was hiccupping, as if something was wrong with it. But still it trundled forward on its caterpillar tracks. The grabber at the front was horribly close.

'He's coming straight at us!' Asha wailed.

'He can't. He won't. Crushing children? Imagine what would happen to him then!'

'Ohhh.' Asha broke free. 'I can't stand it.'

Holly grabbed her arm and dragged her back. 'It's OK!'

The digger coughed, seeming to struggle as it moved from the tarmac onto the long grass and into a tall patch of nettles. Now it crunched over the pile of dry sticks and weeds and grass they'd used as camouflage. It stopped as it hit the log they'd balanced over the deep trench.

'What if it goes straight over the top and carries on?' Noah said. It did seem possible, suddenly.

Zeke aimed another pistol-load of water at the man. It sprayed over his helmet. Toby cheered.

Crack!

The sound of splintering wood echoed out over the Wilderness.

The engine stuttered and died.

The digger tipped to one side: it seemed to hover there, balanced for a second on the edge of the hole.

The man swore loudly, and almost as if in slow motion, the digger toppled into the trench. The orange top of the cab came to rest at a jaunty angle, sticking half out.

'Yay! We did it!' Phoebe shouted.

Everyone cheered and stamped their feet. 'We won! We won! We stopped the digger!'

And then, one by one they went quiet. For a few long

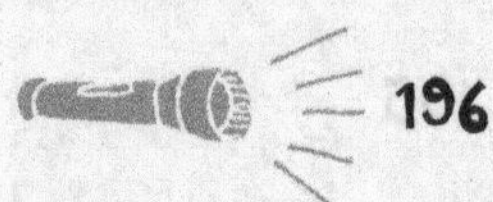

seconds there was silence. No one moved.

Noah noticed birdsong, the chirrup of grasshoppers. A bee buzzed past on its way to the bramble patch, and high in the blue summer sky, an aeroplane left its white vapour trail.

The man didn't move.

'Is he hurt?' Asha whispered. 'Oh no!'

Chapter 25

'He's fine,' Holly said. 'Watch.'

The man climbed awkwardly out of the digger. Water dripped off his helmet. His T-shirt was stained with mud and sweat and potato.

He suddenly looked smaller and very silly.

'OK, lads,' the man said, ankle-deep in mud. 'I suppose you think this is funny. Hahahaha. Satisfied, now? Great joke.'

'*Lads?*' Phoebe exploded. 'We're not *lads!*'

Zeke couldn't stop himself. He fired a final spurt of water. 'Oops,' he said. The man's trousers looked rather wetter than before.

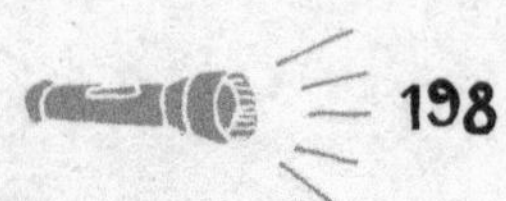

'You little toerag!' The man lunged towards Zeke as if he was about to cuff him round the ears, but Phoebe got there first. She leapt into the trench, grabbed the man's arm, and wouldn't let go.

He shook his arm; she hung on like a monkey. Any minute now and she'd actually bite him.

'*Phoebe!*' Toby and Holly yelled. 'Stop it!"

She let go and fell into the mud, laughing.

Zeke looked a bit sheepish. He'd been—*saved?* By the new girl?

But everything was spiralling out of control and Toby was furious.

Holly stepped forward. 'Sorry about that,' she said. 'She's—new.' It wasn't much of an explanation. 'We're protecting the land. It's ours. We play here. And there's wildlife and birds. Maybe newts. And bats. And you don't have permission to dig, anyway. We had to stop you. It's totally against the law.'

'Totally,' Asha said. 'No one's got planning permission.'

'I've got my instructions,' the man said. 'And it is *against the law*, since you mention it, for you hooligans to get in my way. Obstruction and trespass.'

Toby glared. 'Instructions from whom, exactly?'

'Cheeky blighter,' the man said. 'From Mr Treasure, who is the actual real owner of this bit of derelict land. Hence you lot are guilty of trespass. And now criminal damage, to boot. While I am simply doing my job. What I am paid for. Now scram.'

Noah's head felt as if it would burst. His brain raced. The owner of the land was Mr Treasure? Where had he heard that name before?

The man carried on yelling.

Asha put her hands over her ears. She looked about to cry.

'Go on, all of you. RUN. And take that stupid blimmin' tent with you or I'll dig that up too. Where the heck are your parents? They should be ashamed of you all, running wild like animals.'

The man looked at his digger. He shook his fists. 'I'll have the law on the lot of you. Deliberate sabotage. Malicious forethought and intent.'

Phoebe giggled.

The man tried to climb out, but the sides of the trench were so muddy he kept slipping back. He did look funny,

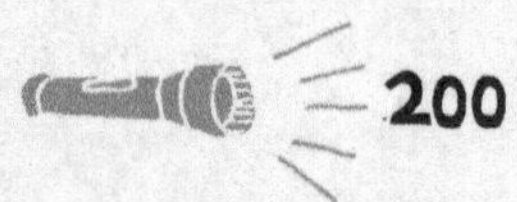

Noah thought, but maybe it wasn't a good idea to laugh at him right now.

Asha and Holly each reached out a hand to help him up.

He scowled. He so did not want their help.

He scrambled up and out of the trench. His face was red and sweaty.

'Are you OK?' Asha asked. 'We didn't mean you to get hurt, honestly. But we had to stop you digging up our beautiful Wilderness.'

'Beautiful?' He spat on the ground. 'This miserable dump?'

'*We* like it,' Holly said. 'It's our place. We've always played here.' She turned on the charm. 'Didn't *you* have a special wild place to play when you were a child?'

He didn't look as if he had *ever* been a child, Noah thought.

The man got his phone out and started tapping in a number.

Noah looked at Holly, and Toby, and the others. What now?

The man spoke into the phone. 'Fred here. Bit of an accident with the mini-digger. Yep. Rough ground. Very

uneven.' He coughed. 'Deep hole. Might need a tow out. No. Yes. Pear Tree Buildings. Nightmare hill. Nope. Okey dokey.'

He hadn't mentioned them.

Of course! The man was *embarrassed* about what had happened. He felt humiliated, because they were children and they'd made a fool out of him. Adults hate that.

Fair enough. They could help him out of a tricky situation. Make a pact. Bargain with him.

'If we all work together, we could get your digger out,' Noah said. 'Long as you promise never to try to dig up our Wilderness ever again.'

The man stared at Noah as if he was totally bonkers.

There was the sound of feet pounding up the street.

Noah turned to look.

Mum was panting up the hill. 'Stop right there!' she yelled.

Did she mean him? Or the man? Noah couldn't tell. Maybe both.

A few steps behind, Anil and Asha's mum clipped up the hill, smartly dressed in her work clothes and high heels. In one hand she held an impressive-looking folder, and in the other, Anil's dad's camera. *Click-click-click.* She took a series of photos of the man, and then the truck, and now the digger.

Noah and the others watched, open-mouthed.

A blue car reversed down Pear Tree Buildings at exactly that moment and slowed to a halt alongside them.

Toby and Holly both stared in astonishment.

'What's *Dad* doing here?' Holly said.

Chapter 26

Toby and Holly's dad lowered the car window. He leaned over to speak to them. 'OK, kids? How's it going?'

He sounded relaxed. 'All right, mate?' He nodded at the digger man, who stood there speechless for the moment, his trousers spattered with mud, his trainers ruined.

Noah saw Mum take in the scene. She sighed deeply.

Oh dear. Trouble ahead.

Natalie ran over and clung onto Mum like a limpet. Mum patted Nat's head absent-mindedly.

Noah looked away, so he wouldn't catch Mum's eye.

Anil and Asha's mum assessed the situation. She put on her serious work voice.

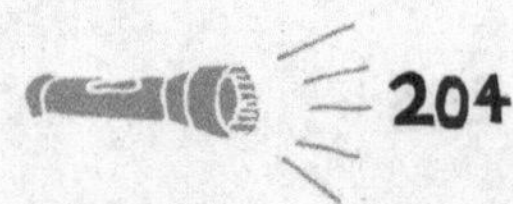

'Dr Jamila Gupta,' she introduced herself to the man. '*Lawyer*. And also local resident. Perhaps you'd like to explain exactly what you are doing here.'

The children watched.

So did the grown-ups.

Anil and Asha's mum was awesome.

The man straightened himself up. 'I'm doing my job,' he said. 'Under instruction. But didn't anticipate—' he coughed—'the exact nature of the ground in question.'

'The ground in question?' Mrs—Dr—Gupta said. 'Meaning?'

'The derelict wasteland due to be flattened. Prior to building works. It's rather steep. And bumpy. With deep holes.'

'But there has been no application for planning, as yet. At least, the residents here have not been informed of such, by individual letter, as required,' Dr Gupta continued. 'And so no one should be flattening the land or removing mature trees. It's an illegal act.'

The man squirmed slightly. 'Not my business,' he said. 'I'm simply doing what I'm told.'

'By whom?'

'Mr Treasure.'

'Ah.'

Toby and Holly's dad spoke up. 'If I may interrupt a moment—it so happens I have been talking about this very matter with the council planning department this morning. I can shed some light—'

'Over a cup of tea, perhaps, in a minute.' Dr Gupta smiled at him. She turned back to the digger man.

'Luckily, no one has been hurt. But I think you will find it is not only against the law but also a breach of safety rules, to bring a digger onto steep land where children are playing—'

The man looked about to explode. But he kept quiet. Dr Gupta had that effect on people.

'And you are?' She waited for him to speak.

'Your name is?' she repeated.

'Fred!' Phoebe piped up.

'Mr Frederick Manners.'

Phoebe giggled. Holly jabbed her in the ribs before she could open her mouth to make a joke.

'I've taken photographs as evidence,' Dr Gupta said. 'I'll be in touch with Mr Treasure shortly. And YOU had better get that digger off the land, and your lorry off our street, as quickly as you can. And wait to hear further *instructions*.'

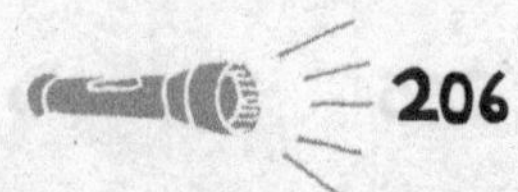

‘I’ve phoned for assistance,’ he mumbled. ‘They’re on their way. I’ll wait in the lorry cab.’

They watched him go.

Toby grinned.

Zeke did the thumbs-up sign.

Anil and Asha high-fived.

‘Hot chocolate? Tea? Second breakfast, everyone?’ Dr Gupta said. ‘Time we all had a little chat.’

Mr Moss was leaning on his gate. He raised his arm in a wobbly kind of salute as the children walked past. ‘Well done! You showed him!’ Mr Moss said. ‘Thinks he can do what he likes.’

Noah stopped.

The others kept on walking down the hill.

‘That weasel, Treasure, he’s being trying to build on this land for years. Greedy, avaricious opportunist,’ Mr Moss said.

‘He owns the land,’ Noah said. ‘You knew all along.’

‘Not much of it, he doesn’t,’ Mr Moss said. ‘Not my bit of garden. With the greenhouse and all my lovely plants, back in the day.’

Noah looked across at the greenhouse.

Of course. Mr Moss's garden.

Something was creaking round his brain. The name. Treasure. Where had he seen it, before?

'Noah!' Holly yelled. Come on!'

'Can I come and see you later?' Noah said. 'I've got some things I need to ask you. Urgently.'

'Any time you like.' Mr Moss tried to laugh, but it made him cough. 'I'm not going anywhere in a hurry!'

*

Noah and the others squeezed onto the sofa in Anil and Asha's front room. All except Phoebe, who had made a dash for home. Toby bagged the armchair.

They sipped at mugs of hot chocolate, trying not to spill any on the red rug or the polished wooden floor. After the excitement of their victory, they had now all gone rather quiet.

Noah looked around. There were millions of books on shelves that went from the floor to the ceiling. A collection of small china birds was arranged along the stone mantelpiece either side of a vase full of roses. It was all dead posh. They never came in here, normally. They'd go into the kitchen, or to Asha or Anil's rooms upstairs. But Asha and Anil's mum had ushered them into the sitting room and made them sit down.

The parents were talking together in the kitchen.

Noah was thinking about what Mr Moss had said. He needed to find out more, soon as this was over.

Dr Gupta came back into the front room.

It was a bit crowded. Toby got up and sat on the floor.

Mum, and Toby and Holly's mum and dad, stood in the doorway to listen.

Dr Gupta sat down in the armchair. 'Thank you, Toby. Now,' she said. 'We want to hear *your* version of what exactly has been going on. Who would like to start?'

Asha spoke up first. 'We've been working together to protect the Wilderness. There was a notice—about selling it, and building on it.'

'But we can't let that happen,' Anil added. 'Obviously. And we found about the Wildlife laws, cos a man tried to cut down the trees, and it turns out it was illegal then because of the birds' nests, but it's not now cos today's July 31st.'

'So one of us should be on lookout watch right now,' Toby said. 'The tree man might arrive any minute.'

‘I will—,’ Noah volunteered.

Mum cleared her throat. ‘No, Noah. You stay put. But I’ll pop my head out and check what’s happening in the street.’

‘We won’t be long,’ Dr Gupta said. ‘We need to talk to all of you children together. So, carry on, please.’

‘And then we found out about the digger coming, and we had to stop it. So we camped out all night, so we’d be ready in the morning. We are a proper protest with banners and everything. You have to *fight* to save what you love,’ Zeke said.

Dr Gupta frowned slightly. ‘So, you attacked the digger?’

‘Not exactly,’ Asha said. ‘We put banners in the trees, and made some traps—and the digger fell in a hole . . .’

Toby and Holly’s dad grinned widely from the doorway. Their mum, standing next to him, had her arms wrapped tight round her middle, as if she was trying to stop herself from laughing out loud. She rocked slightly with the effort.

Asha folded her hands in her lap. ‘The man wasn’t hurt.’ Her voice came out very clear and precise; Noah could tell she was a bit nervous.

‘We haven’t done anything wrong,’ Holly said. ‘The man with the digger was breaking the law.’

Dr Gupta smiled. ‘Yes. You’re right about that. And none

of us wants houses on the wild area, with its lovely old trees and all the butterflies and birds. It would change this street entirely. The street isn't wide enough for any more traffic, in any case. And it's wonderful to have that space for you children to play. But we have to be careful, and not take the law into our own hands. The man-trap was a little dangerous, and now we know someone *does* own the land, we have to think what that means. Strictly speaking, you were all trespassing. The tent will have to come down, too.'

'We've *always* played there. It's *our* Wilderness.' Toby was still furious.

'Well, the good news is, your dad's been finding out some useful things about that, Toby.'

Toby and Holly's dad waved a folder of papers.

'Plus, you children are right: no planning permission for digging up trees or for building houses has been granted, yet. Plus all of us living in the street should, by rights, have had a letter about both the tree-cutting and the digger. So there are wrongs on both sides.'

Mum put her head round the door. 'Truck and digger and man have all gone!' she said. 'And there's no sign of a tree man. Sorry to interrupt.'

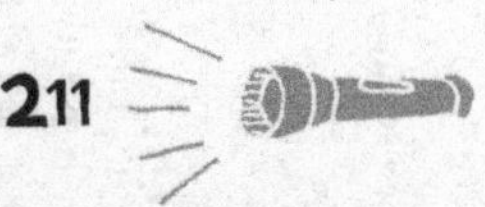

'Yay!' Zeke gave a muted cheer.

Noah squirmed with the effort of sitting still and listening to Dr Gupta's long speeches. His brain hurt, like it did after a day at school when he had been cooped up inside a classroom too long.

'We've just about finished here,' Dr Gupta said. 'All that's left to say is, the really important next step is to stop any planning application for building houses from being successful. I know how to help you do that. And I can make sure the owner knows we're on his case. Stop any more illegal nonsense with diggers or tree surgeons.'

Zeke slurped up the last dregs of chocolate with his straw.

Anil and Asha grinned at the disgusting noise. They weren't allowed to do that, normally.

Toby's dad spoke up. 'OK. So, we'll get the tent down, and then all gather at Toby and Holly's house and I'll show you the papers I've dug out, about the street, and the land. First, though, all hands on deck. Get your sleeping stuff out and we'll take down that tent.'

*

Toby's dad made them all do a share of the work. The canvas had to be shaken out and folded in exactly the way he said.

The metal poles folded up and went into a special bag. The tent pegs went into another, small bag. They each had to be cleaned of earth first. Toby's dad was very particular.

Everyone was exhausted. They sat down on the logs around the ashes of last night's fire.

'Are you sure the digger man won't be back?' Holly asked her dad.

'Quite sure. Dr Gupta has all the legal facts. Nothing can happen now, unless the owner gets planning permission. There has to be a council meeting to decide that, and the council have to tell everyone affected by it—the people who live in this street—when that is. And we'll go along and present our case against it. You children will all do a terrific job, I know.'

Toby kicked a tree stump.

'Come back for some lemonade, and I can show you the maps and papers I found,' Toby's dad said.

'Got to go now,' Zeke mumbled. 'Laters.' He sloped off home.

'I'll be there in a minute,' Noah said. 'Got to do something first.'

Chapter 27

The only sign of the digger truck was a spattering of mud on the road and the ridges left by the caterpillar tracks on the edge of the grass.

Crow swooped down from the ash trees and landed on the greenhouse roof.

Noah still had that trapped feeling in his chest he got sometimes at school. It made him want to run and climb. Or fly, if only he could. How wonderful to able to flap your wings and take off, like Crow.

Once, on holiday, Grandpa had taken Noah sailing. The water was calm when they set off, but the wind got up when they were out in the estuary. It filled the sail and blew the

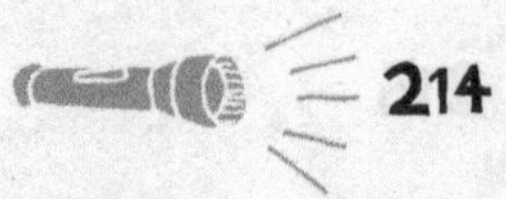

boat fast and free right out into the open sea, where the big waves lifted the small boat up and dropped it back, up and back, over and over. Grandpa had been scared, he told Noah afterwards, but Noah had simply laughed with the excitement and thrill of it. He'd loved the sound of the wind in the sails and the waves slap-slapping under the bows as the boat scudded along. That was the closest feeling to actual flying he'd had.

He had been happy and free as a bird that day.

Maybe that's what he'd do, one day. Learn to sail. Go on an adventure.

Right now, he had to talk to Mr Moss again, and find out more about Mr Treasure.

*

Noah had never been inside Mr Moss's house before. He took a deep breath and knocked on the front door. The paint was peeling off. No one had cleaned the glass for a long time.

Mr Moss opened the door almost immediately. 'Come in,' he said. He peered over Noah's head. 'Anyone else coming in with you? No? Put kettle on, lad, if you like, for tea. We'll leave the door ajar so your mum knows you're safe.'

‘All right,’ Noah said. ‘I can make *you* a cup of tea, if you want. I don’t like tea.’

Mr Moss didn’t seem to hear. He shouted instructions to Noah from his front room. The kitchen was in the same place as Noah’s kitchen, at the back. It was funny, the way the houses all followed the same pattern of rooms, but seemed so different inside. Nothing had changed in Mr Moss’s house in ninety years, Noah reckoned. He made tea in a pot (no tea bags, he had to guess how much to spoon in) and found milk in a jug in the fridge. He put it all on the tray with a picture of an owl on it and carried it through.

‘Lovely job,’ Mr Moss said. ‘Now, how can I help?’

‘What you said, about Mr Treasure. And the land. That he owns some of it, but not your bit. What did you mean?’

‘Ah. Well.’ Mr Moss settled himself back in his chair. He took a sip of tea.

‘We have to go back a bit, first, to *Mavis* Treasure.’

Noah sighed. This was going to take a long time.

‘Mavis lived in number one Pear Tree Buildings a long time ago. More than—let’s see—eighty years ago. She bought the land opposite these houses from the farmer who owned all the land round here in the olden days.

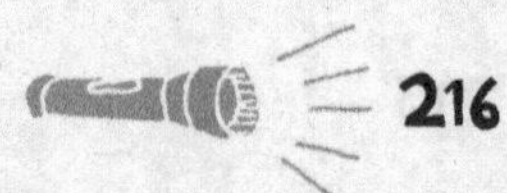

'Anyway, maybe Mavis Treasure thought the land would be worth something, or she had some notion of building on it, but she never did. Instead, she rented it out in strips, to the neighbours who wanted to grow things. Like allotment gardens. People grew their own veg, back in those days. It saved on the expense, like. We paid her for the use, same as people used to pay the farm before. Ground rent. Not much. A few pounds a year.'

It felt to Noah like that moment when at last he found the piece of blue to finish the sky on one of Nana's jigsaws. *Two pounds and ten shillings. Ground rent. M. Treasure*. Of course! That old paper receipt he'd found in the greenhouse. It all began to make sense.

'When she died, her son inherited her house, though he never lived in it: too small for the likes of him. He inherited the few bits and pieces of land that Mavis didn't sell off before she died, too.' Mr Moss stopped to cough. 'Seems that there was a legal right for people to buy their strip of land, after so many years of paying rent. Lots didn't bother. Too tricky, gardening on such a slope and with all the brambles. Plus the bogs and springs. In a wet winter, they come up all over the place.'

Noah was keeping up so far, just about.

'Anyway, some of the people DID buy their strip. We did. Couple of doors down at number ten, I think they bought theirs—the people before the ones living there now, I mean. No one's gardened it for years. And mebbe the folks at number fourteen or fifteen, before you came along, Noah, and number seven and eight. It's such a long time ago, I forget. And the land gradually went back to the wild again, like land does, if humans leave it be.'

The cogs in Noah's brain turned and connected and turned some more, as he fitted the pieces of information together.

Mr Moss carried on. 'I don't know about those houses at the very top of the street. Perhaps it's the land opposite them that's up for grabs.' He looked at Noah. 'You can ask that pretty lass who's just moved in. It'll be in the house deeds. That's the legal papers, with all the facts and history of a house, going back over the years. There'll be information from the land registry, too, about who owns the land opposite.'

'So, do you still own your strip of garden, Mr Moss?' Noah leaned closer to listen.

Mr Moss slurped his tea and spilled some in the saucer.

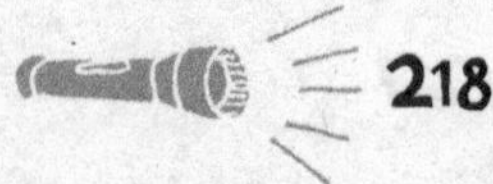

'Yes. It didn't cost much. We put up the greenhouse, and grew tomatoes and veg, and picked the pears off the old orchard trees. But it was too much work, once my lovely wife died, and me legs got bad . . . so it's all gone wild, now.

'I like to see you, Noah, watching the wildlife, and playing outside with your friends, like we did way back when I were a lad. And with that young crow.'

Noah nodded. 'He trusts me more now,' he said. 'Follows me about. And I made a pond,' he said. 'There's water bugs and a dragonfly already.'

Mr Moss nodded. 'Good lad. All the wild things need water. The deer, too. That'll keep it coming back.'

Noah stared.

'You've seen it too?'

'Once or twice, very early morning.' Mr Moss's pale blue eyes twinkled. 'Isn't it lovely? So wild, and shy, and fragile.'

Noah nodded.

'It's not rare, though,' Noah said. 'It's not on the list of rare species.'

'Shame,' Mr Moss said. 'Even so, you might get them wildlife people interested; there's charities and such-like, for protecting nature.'

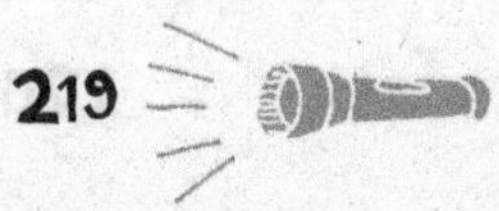

'Anil and Asha's mum's going to help us tell the council planning people about why the Wilderness is important.'

'She's a good 'un,' Mr Moss said. 'Clever lady.'

They sat in silence for a while.

Mr Moss finished his tea and rested the cup back on the saucer. His hands shook so much the cup rattled. 'So, lad, the long and short of the matter is this: greedy-guts Mr Treasure may *try* to sell that top bit of land off to developers, or try to get planning permission to build another few houses himself, but he won't succeed.'

'How do you know that?' Noah asked.

Mr Moss's face creased into a smile. 'He tried before and he didn't then, and he won't now, because *you* and your friends are going to stop him! Like you told me. I'm relying on you, Noah. I know you can do it.'

Noah's stomach lurched. For one teeny second, he'd thought Mr Moss was going to give him the answer: an actual reason why the Wilderness would be all right.

But no.

Disappointed, Noah stood up. 'I've got to go, now. So, where does Mr Treasure live?'

'That I don't know, Noah. I've got no dealings with that

weasel any more, thank goodness. Not round here, for sure. Brighton? Birmingham, or Bristol? Bolton, maybe. I've a notion it began with B.'

'OK. Thanks, Mr Moss,' Noah said.

Mr Moss couldn't help much, but he had done his best. He was kind, and so very old. Maybe a bit lonely, living by himself. And strangely, it wasn't that hard to imagine Mr Moss being a boy, like Noah, playing outside on the Wilderness, watching the wildlife and feeding the birds.

*

Crow was waiting for him in the pear tree. He flew down and landed on the pavement.

'Hello, Crow!'

Crow put his head on one side, listening. He hopped closer to Noah.

'So, what do you think about all this?' Noah asked.

Caw!

'You *don't* think, that's what. You just *are*. And you're hungry again.' Noah rummaged in his pocket and pulled out a handful of mixed seeds. He held his palm flat.

Tap, tap, tap, his beak pecked the seed from Noah's hand.

'You're getting big,' Noah said. Carefully, he held out his

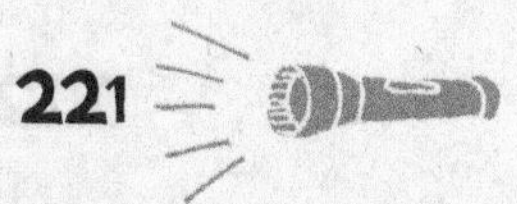

other hand to see if Crow would let him stroke his feathery head.

No. Not yet.

'I'm going to Toby and Holly's, now, to see what their dad's found out.'

Crow flew away, as if he understood.

*

Down at number seven, it was almost like last summer, when Toby's dad still lived there. Toby and Holly's mum was making coffee; Toby and Holly's dad was sitting at the kitchen table with a load of papers spread out before him, with Toby and Holly either side of him, and Anil, Asha, and Nat were squeezed along the bench opposite them.

Noah hovered in the doorway, taking it all in. It was good that Toby and Holly's mum and dad were speaking to each other now.

'Hi, Noah!' everyone chorused.

'Lemonade, Noah?' Toby and Holly's mum cleared a space among the papers and put down the pot of coffee.

Noah shook his head. 'I'm all right, thanks.'

'Dad went to the council offices,' Toby said. 'Found out some cool stuff about the Wilderness.' He spread out a big

sheet of paper. 'See? This is our street, when it was first built.'

Noah peered over his shoulder at the photocopied pages. It was an old map. The date 1884 was handwritten in the bottom left-hand corner.

Toby pointed to the streets. 'Look, this is Pear Tree Buildings, and behind here, see, it says Maycombe Farm, and this is our row of houses, when they were first built. Back then, there weren't all the other streets and houses around here.'

Noah nodded.

'And here, the opposite side of our street, is the Wilderness. But see, in the olden days it was divided up into strips that line up with the houses opposite. As if they were long, thin gardens once upon a time.'

Noah knew he should say something, right now, about what Mr Moss had told him. But he kept quiet.

Toby's dad leaned forwards to study the map again. 'Perhaps that old farm—Maycombe Farm—owned all the land round here, and had orchards of fruit trees, which is how our street got its name. Interesting, eh?'

Toby's mum joined them at the table. 'It's fun, finding out the stories about our houses. Imagine, back then in 1884,

the city was less spread out, and we'd have been right on the edge, with fields all round. Woods, too: see?' She pointed at a shaded area on the map. 'Plenty of places to play and have adventures.'

Asha pulled out another of the papers. It was some sort of legal document, with hardly any spaces and too dense and complicated for Noah even to pretend to read it. 'This is interesting too, about land ownership, from the Land Registry . . .'

Holly had gone into the front room. She started playing the piano. She hadn't done that for ages. The piano was out of tune.

Noah had had enough of all the talking and long words. He escaped from the kitchen, and went through to listen to Holly.

She grinned at him. 'Good. Now you're here you can do the top part.'

She looked much happier today, Noah thought. So did Toby.

'I've forgotten how to play it,' he said. 'Show me the notes.'

Holly played the top part to remind him how. He practised with two fingers. She did the more complicated chords

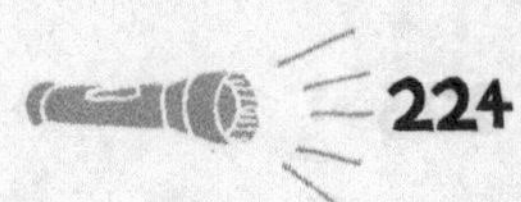

of the lower part with both hands and the proper fingers. After a few goes, they sounded quite good together.

'Are you OK?' Holly said. 'You seem—'

'What?'

'I dunno. A bit preoccupied. Not like usual.'

Could he tell Holly?

He might as well try. If anyone could understand, it would be Holly.

'All this stuff—your dad's map, and something Mr Moss said about the land . . .'

Holly rested her arms on the keyboard. 'Yes?'

'Mr Moss said people used to garden on the bits of land opposite their houses.'

Holly listened.

Noah tried again. 'If the Wilderness was gardens, it isn't the Wilderness any more. Not wild.'

Holly sighed. 'Oh, Noah.'

'And now all the adults are talking about the Wilderness, it isn't *ours* any more either. I don't like it.'

'We're still in charge, Noah. It was *us* who stopped the digger. You and Toby scared off those teenagers. *We* built the dens and man-traps. The Wilderness is just the same as

it always has been, all grown-over and brambly and stinging nettle-y. No one gardens it; they haven't for years and years. And that's why all the insects and other creatures have come, too. And that's what we have to protect.'

'There's more . . .'

Bit by bit, Noah poured out to Holly everything Mr Moss had said, about the strips of garden, and paying rent, and then buying pieces of the land. He told her about the old map, how it actually showed lines dividing the Wilderness into long thin strips.

'If everyone finds out, then what? They might put up fences round their bit. Build sheds and garages. Grow flowers and cut the grass and make it all tame and safe and boring. And all the wild creatures will disappear . . . and we won't be able to play there, either.'

Holly lowered the piano lid. 'I don't think so. We know most of the people in the street. They're too busy for gardening and they won't want to put up fences. Don't you see, Noah? This might really help us. If it means everyone has a right to buy the bit of Wilderness opposite their house, we can get everyone to agree to keep it like it is. We could get the whole street to join in and help protect the Wilderness.

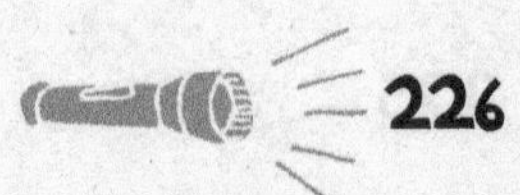

We can all be on the same side. You should tell Anil and Asha's mum. And Dad. He really wants to help us. Mum's pleased.'

Noah nodded. He hesitated, not sure if he should ask. 'So, what's happening with your mum and dad?'

'He and Mum have been talking more, because of the Wilderness. It's like they're friends again.'

'Good.'

'And Dad's going to take Toby and me camping.'

'You can't go away now!'

'Not now; at the end of August.'

Holly's mum called from the kitchen. 'Play us another duet, Holly and Noah.'

Holly looked at Noah. He shook his head.

'Later,' Holly yelled back. 'We're going outside now.'

'Come on,' she said to Noah. 'Cheer up. Hide-and-seek? Murder in the dark, in the bramble den? Kick-the-can?'

Anil, Asha, and Nat were already running out onto the street to play.

'Someone should still be on lookout,' Noah said, 'just in case.'

He stopped at the kitchen door. 'Coming out, Tobes?'

‘Nah. Dad and me are going to town to find out more stuff. I’ll see you later. We’re all meeting at four in the bramble den, remember.’ Toby didn’t even look up.

Noah left him to it. He was happy for Toby. Really, he was. Working to save the Wilderness was helping him get closer to his dad again. It was helping his mum and dad talk more, too. That was really good.

Chapter 28

Toby was brimming with news.

He'd been to the council offices in town with his dad, and the library too. They'd discovered the date for the next planning applications meeting. They'd actually seen the outline plans for building five houses on the Wilderness. Mr Treasure had made the planning application now. Really he wanted to sell the land to a developer. Having the planning consent would mean he could ask for an extra big amount of money. He was a greedy man. All he cared about was money. He didn't live in the street; he didn't care about the people whose lives it would affect. And he certainly didn't care about possible bats or newts, or butterflies and moths and beetles.

Or wild places for children to play.

Noah felt more worried and sad and defeated, the more Toby said.

It all sounded so . . . official. It was all in the hands of the grown-ups. What difference could they make, to all that?

'So,' Toby said, 'August 5th. That's the date of the Planning Committee meeting. We will all go to it, in the Town Hall.

'Asha and Anil's mum is helping us prepare a case with evidence and legal stuff, so that's brilliant. At the meeting, we all have to stand up together at the front and say why we object to the plans for buildings on the Wilderness. Dad's found out about something called the council's development plan, which says they have to protect green spaces in urban areas and provide allotments. So that's good.'

'Mum says we can talk about the wildlife living here, even if it isn't rare, and the importance of keeping mature trees, and why the land should be protected as it is,' Anil said.

'And she's doing some research with the Land Registry about who owns the land, exactly, because it seems to be more complicated than everyone thinks.' Asha smiled. She was getting more confident about speaking out.

Holly looked at Noah: a sort of question on her face.

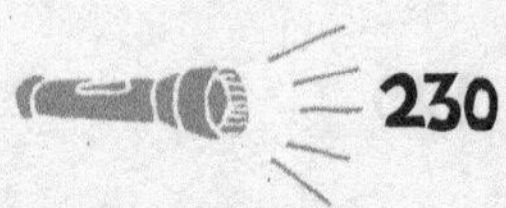

'I know some stuff too,' Noah said. 'Mr Moss told me.'

Holly nodded encouragingly. 'You must tell Asha's mum what he said, Noah.'

There was a scuffle, and loud giggles.

Natalie and Phoebe emerged into the den, bits of twig and pink petals caught in their hair from crawling along the tunnel.

'Sorry we're late!' Nat said. 'We forgot.'

Everyone shuffled round to make room.

Phoebe grinned. She crossed her legs, then stretched them out and twiddled her feet to show off her gold sparkly pumps.

'Pretty shoes!' Asha smiled at Phoebe. But her smile froze.

Noah saw what Asha had just noticed. Phoebe held a small red and gold bowl in her hand, with sweets inside.

'That's Asha's bowl!' he blurted out.

'Oh! Is it? I found it,' Phoebe said innocently. 'I didn't know it was yours.' She handed it to Asha. 'There you are, then. You can have all the sweets too, if you like.'

Asha said thank you very quietly. She shared the sweets round.

Noah didn't want one.

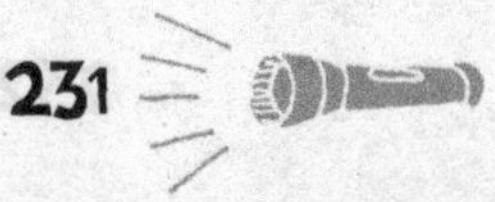

He was sure Phoebe was lying about the bowl, like she had about the bell. She'd nicked them both from Asha's den that day, he was almost certain.

'Anyway,' Toby said, 'let's get on with it. We need to think what we want to say at the council meeting, and what evidence we can take along. Holly first.'

'I still think it's about showing what we love about the Wilderness, and making other people care too.'

'Well, how?'

'We can show my photos,' Anil said. 'I can make, like, a film, or a PowerPoint presentation with all the images blown up big on a screen.'

'And get a petition with signatures from everyone in the street,' Zeke said. 'Create a Facebook page.'

Noah felt himself going smaller and smaller inside.

'How about we draw a *huge*, beautiful map of the Wilderness, with drawings and photos stuck on, really bright and colourful? A really creative, arty sort of map picture,' Holly suggested.

'Oh yes! I can make butterflies and use net for wings and we can use gold material, and stick leaves and feathers on and use Phoebe's glitter pens; please can we, Phebes?' Nat said.

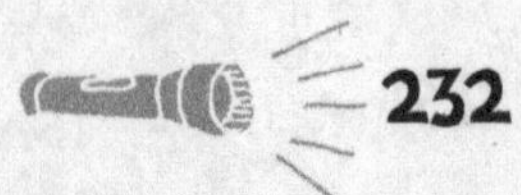

Phoebe nodded.

'Don't go too mad,' Toby said. 'It's supposed to be a map.'

'It can still be beautiful,' Holly said. 'That's the whole point.'

'I could come in costume,' Zeke said. 'I can borrow one of Dani's animal ones from the stage props at her college. Expect you could all have one, if you wanted.'

'Like what?'

'All sorts. Lion, tiger, polar bear, fox, wolf, squirrel, monkey.'

Anil snorted. 'You can't go as a lion or a monkey! It has to be something that you can see for real in the Wilderness.'

'Deer or squirrel, then.'

'Deer?'

'Noah's seen one.'

'When? Why didn't you say? That's really cool!'

'You should tell everyone about the deer at the meeting, Noah!'

'No!' Noah went hot. Talking too much about the deer seemed to take away the magic, somehow—and it wasn't rare, or anything that would count in a meeting . . .

'You could dress up as the deer!' Zeke said.

'No thanks,' Noah said quickly. The thought of dressing up, like in the school play, made him sweat with fear.

'I'll write a script of what to say, to outline our case why no one should ever build here.' Toby picked up a pen and started making notes on his clipboard.

'Make a list. Numbered points.'

'We should take the signs and banners we made, too, so we look like a proper protest when the TV come to take photos outside the council offices.'

'The TV won't be there! Don't be daft, Zeke!'

'Why not? Why don't we ask them? Local TV and radio and the paper and we can put it on Twitter.'

'You're not allowed on Twitter.'

'No, but Dani is. She's on it all the time. Facebook, Instagram. We can tell the world.'

It was all getting a bit bonkers, Noah thought. But maybe they were right. Maybe that's what they had to do. Just as long as he didn't have to say anything. On the day, he could stay here, quietly, looking after the Wilderness in his own way, and let the others get on with it.

'You've gone quiet, Noah,' Toby said. 'What will you do?'

'You could draw some creatures to go on our map,' Holly

suggested. 'You'd be good at that. Birds, grasshoppers, beetles.' She was being kind, helping him out.

Anil spoke up. 'But I've already got photos of all those—'

'Shut up!' Asha said.

'I know!' Anil changed tack. 'What would be really brilliant, would be if you came to the meeting with Crow perched on your shoulder, Noah!'

'Oh yes!'

'Wow, that would be so a–maz-ing!'

'Everyone would sit up and take notice, then.'

It was a brilliant idea, everyone agreed.

'No way,' Noah said. 'Never. Crow isn't a pet. I'd never take him inside a building. In any case, he wouldn't let me. Is the meeting over?' He didn't wait for an answer. He was already crawling out of the den, along the bramble tunnel, out into the warm air.

He climbed the lookout tree and sat for ages on the wooden platform, his stomach churning, his mind blank.

Crow landed nearby, on the rowan tree. Noah knew it was a rowan tree because he'd looked it up. It had berries in the winter. Its other name was *mountain ash*. They grew wild in places like Scotland. But someone must have planted this one.

One of the people who had once lived in the street, and gardened here.

Urgh. Why had he never thought about all these signs that the Wilderness had once been gardens and orchards, and owned by someone? He felt stupid.

Crow flew over and landed right beside Noah's foot.

Noah fished into his pocket and found some seed.

Noah kept very still. He held his arm out straight, the seed safe inside his closed fist.

Crow flew up. He perched on Noah's arm, cocked his shiny dark head and looked right at him.

'So, you are getting braver, Crow.' Noah talked very softly, the way Crow liked. 'Brave enough to let me touch you, yet?'

Crow moved his head, as if he was listening.

Noah slowly stretched out his other arm, and moved it closer, slowly, slowly, until he was touching the bird's head with one finger. He waited, holding his breath. He stroked Crow's head.

He opened his hand out, and Crow pecked up the seed.

Noah let out his breath. Wow. That was amazing. Crow trusted him at last.

And then the moment was over. Natalie came running

through the grass, making a racket, scaring everything. Crow flapped up and away.

*

Noah watched from his perch as all his friends spread out over the Wilderness, taking photos, and drawing, and mucking about. Holly, Nat, and Phoebe posed for a photograph together in the pirate ship den. Asha skipped over the road and inside her house.

Toby's dad was back, talking to Toby at the edge of the road; they crouched together over Toby's clipboard. Toby was writing things down.

He saw Zeke in his front garden, talking into a mobile phone. Noah guessed he was chatting to his sister Dani about the costumes, or Twitter, or something.

Phoebe wandered slowly up the road arm in arm with Nat. He expected them to go all the way up to number thirty, but they stopped instead at number twelve.

Mr Moss was at his gate.

Noah watched.

Phoebe and Nat talked to him for a while at the gate, then followed Mr Moss inside his house.

Noah's heart sank. What were they up to *now?*

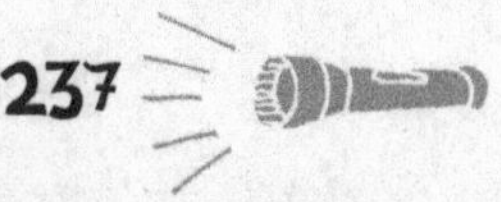

Chapter 29

The planning permission meeting loomed closer. Noah could think of nothing else.

Everyone was busy, getting ready. Holly, Asha, Anil, and Nat seemed to enjoy all the making, and photographing, and writing things down, and getting organized, and practising speeches, and getting signatures.

All the parents wanted to come to the meeting. Toby's dad and Anil and Asha's mum were preparing evidence to back up the children. Noah had finally told Dr Gupta about Mr Moss's strip of garden. She'd been really pleased. She had gone to talk to Mr Moss herself, to find out more.

Noah drew a picture of a lesser water boatman for Holly's

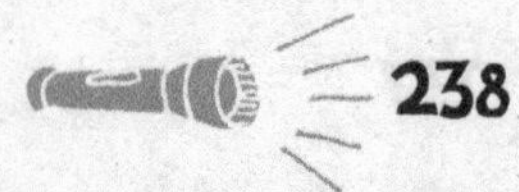

map; it came out a bit big, but he wanted to show all the details, including the bubble of air. He helped Anil photograph the different species of dragonfly and damselflies visiting the pond.

He still insisted he wouldn't say anything at the meeting. He would come along, if he had to. But not speak.

'Why not?' Toby kept asking. 'You're just being stubborn, Noah. Just because you don't *like* doing something, doesn't mean you shouldn't do it. What's the matter with you?'

Noah couldn't explain. He spent most of the days up the tree, on the lookout platform, with Crow. He felt lonely. They'd stopped playing man-hunt, or kick-the-can. They hadn't made a fire since the night they'd camped out. It was as if all the things he loved had been taken away already.

Toby stayed over at his dad's flat by himself for the first time.

*

The next morning, Holly came to visit Noah. She climbed up the tree, and settled next to him on the wooden platform. It creaked, and swayed a bit.

'Whoops,' Holly said. 'Is it safe?'

Noah nodded. 'For two, should be.'

Holly handed him a plastic bag. 'For you,' she said. 'I just picked them.'

Noah peered inside the bag. Blackberries. 'Thanks.' He waited. He guessed Holly had something else she wanted to tell him.

They ate the blackberries between them. The juice stained their fingers and mouths dark red, like blood.

Holly flipped through the pages of his nature book. She put it back on the wooden platform. She shifted round, to get comfortable.

Noah thought about watching damselflies earlier this morning—two, with *iridescent* blue bodies and *translucent* wings. Those were two new words he'd found in Mr Moss's book. He'd been looking at it more and more. The good thing about a book was, you could take it outside and read it up a tree.

'Phoebe asked Mr Moss to sign Zeke's petition, and he got talking, and then she said she wanted to record him telling old stories about when he first lived in the street, and about the land, and so he told her and Nat about his garden and the greenhouse, and buying his strip of land, and then he said she should check her house deeds to see

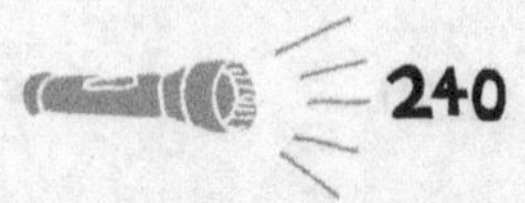

if she owned the land opposite her house, too.' Holly took a big breath.

'And does she?'

'No. Because her mum doesn't own the house, they're just renting it. So they can't look at the house deeds.'

Noah felt relieved. He didn't want Phoebe owning a bit of his Wilderness.

'But there's something much more exciting!' Holly said. Her eyes were shining now. She looked ready to burst.

'What?'

'We can! Dad's seen the deeds for our house, a big folder of old papers with old-fashioned writing going back more than one hundred years and there's proof that the strip of land opposite our house was rented out as garden, and then bought for two hundred and fifty pounds. So it's actually ours!' Holly hugged him she was so happy.

Noah squirmed.

'Isn't it good? And now your mum and dad can check your house deeds, and so can Asha and Anil's parents, and Zeke's mum.' Holly could hardly keep still she was so excited. The wooden platform rocked as she jiggled about. 'Oh Noah, why aren't you more excited? It means our bits of the Wilderness are safe, don't you see? And none of us will put up fences on sheds or make it neat and boring; it will stay wild. It will be properly ours.'

'But what about all the other people? And the land at the top is still going to get built on. *Five* houses, Toby said.'

'We're going to stop that happening too, Noah. That's why we have to be at the planning meeting, all of us together, and *speak*. Please, Noah. You know so much about all the wild creatures, and it matters to you so much, you *have* to say something. You are the most important person of all.'

Noah was silent.

'Even Phoebe is joining in now. Why won't you?'

Noah couldn't explain. Not even to Holly. He'd tried before. It would be like when he was in the nativity play in reception class, and again in year four, when Mrs Harris made him stand on stage in the class performance, and he forgot everything he was supposed to say or do. Or reading out loud in class, when the words got mixed-up and blurred and jumped about, and nothing made any sense. He'd be sick. In public.

Or worse.

'Think about it,' Holly said. 'Promise me, Noah.'

She climbed down to the branch below.

'Please?'

Noah hated to let down Holly. She was kind. And brave. And clever. And of course he wanted to save the Wilderness.

More than anyone.

More than anything.

So he made a huge effort, and nodded. But she couldn't see that, of course, from the branch below.

'OK, Holly.' His voice came out thin and hollow. 'I'll think about it.'

He watched her jump the last bit, and run up the hill towards the pirate den.

Holly had hoisted the flag; it flapped in the breeze, a skull and crossbones. And . . . Noah felt disappointed, and cross, and sad, all at the same time . . . Crow was sitting right on the top of the broom-handle mast, watching Phoebe and Nat below, beady-eyed, as they opened the biscuit tin.

Even Crow had deserted him.

Monday 4th August

Chapter 30

It was the night before the big council planning meeting. Everything was ready.

They'd done a rehearsal earlier in the day. Noah watched, but he didn't join in any of the talking.

Noah lay in bed in his attic, going over it all in his mind.

Holly and Nat had drawn their map of the Wilderness, with pictures of all the lovely things that were there, like a treasure map. It was extra big, on the back of some wall-paper, so they could unroll it at the meeting and everyone in the room would be able to see. They'd drawn each den in detail—the pirate ship, Anil and Asha's beautiful tepee, Zach's rough wooden structure, Toby's trench, and Noah's lookout tree. The pond, the ash trees, and the birds' nests were all painted in. They'd coloured in patches for nettles and brambles, sketched the bees and beetles, butterflies and moths that lived there. Natalie had painted a damselfly with her new watercolour paints from Nana—a present for being so brave when she broke her arm.

Noah's picture was part of it, too: the water boatman bug, drawn in microscopic detail from life, but not to scale. Holly had cut it out and stuck it next to the pond, and she'd drawn a magnifying lens around it, to show why it was so big.

Anil put all the photographs he had taken onto his mum's laptop and turned it into a posh presentation. It flicked through the images at ten-second intervals. Asha added some words.

Even Zeke's squirrel costume was brilliant. He had a huge bushy tail, russet brown with a white tip. His sister Dani had promised to bring over her face paints, to give him a squirrelly face.

Phoebe seemed to have calmed down, now she was more a part of the gang. She put notes through the door of every house in the street with the date of the council Planning Committee meeting.

Anil had printed out photos and put them in a folder that they would pass round to all the people in the meeting: one of Mr Moss, two showing the digger in the trench, with their protest signs leant against it; lots more of birds and nests, insects and butterflies; trees and flowers.

And one of Noah and Crow. Noah hadn't realized at the time that Anil had photographed that moment. He hadn't known anyone was watching.

In the photo, Crow was perched on Noah's outstretched arm, his head turned, so he was looking straight at Noah. You could see this sort of look, between the two of them. As if they understood each other.

Wild bird. Boy. Wilderness behind.

It made shivers go down his spine.

Anyway, the plan was, Toby and Holly would do most of the talking, with Anil taking over when it came to the presentation on the computer. Phoebe would introduce her recording of Mr Moss. Zeke would hand round the extra photos, dressed as a squirrel. Phoebe, Natalie and Holly would hold up the map-picture, so everyone could see it. Toby and Holly's dad, and Anil and Asha's mum would drive them down to the Town Hall and be back-up adults for giving evidence. Noah and Nat's mum and dad would sit in the audience, ready to applaud or heckle or do whatever was necessary.

So, there was no need for Noah to worry. He didn't have to speak. He could sit at the back and watch, Holly said, if he really couldn't bear to stand up at the front. But he had to come along.

*

Noah couldn't sleep. He leaned over to see the time on his clock on the bedside table. Eleven thirty-five.

An owl hooted, answered by another.

Noah got out of bed and pushed the skylight window wide.

Traffic still roared along the dual carriageway; the usual city sounds of sirens and traffic hummed and shrilled. The streetlights spread their sodium-yellow glow over the city. Shouts and voices echoed up as the pub emptied out. A car alarm went off. A dog barked, on and on.

But if he blocked out the streetlights with one hand, he could see the dome of navy sky arcing above him, studded with stars. And down below, there was another small patch of darkness.

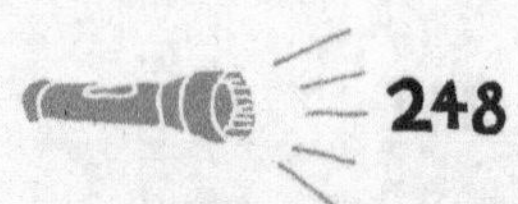

That dark, hidden space, in the middle of it all, just a stone's throw from his home. Even now, deep in the dark, anything might be happening there.

Beetles and spiders and frogs and mice scurrying through the undergrowth.

Bats flitting between the trees and bushes, catching moths.

Tawny owls calling from high in the ash trees.

And maybe his deer, stepping softly through the dew-wet grass, watching everything with its deep dark eyes, ready to run at the slightest sound.

His heart pounded, imagining all the adults talking about his Wilderness at the meeting in the Town Hall, poring over the pros and cons of building five houses. People who knew nothing about what it was really like, or what would be lost forever.

He climbed back into bed.

Still he couldn't settle.

He checked the time again. Twelve-fifteen.

Ten to one.

His head was hot. Perhaps he was ill. Perhaps he'd have to stay at home tomorrow after all.

One twenty-five.

He was still too hot. He thought of the cool of the air outside. The damp grass. The night smells; moonlight casting shadows over the Wilderness.

He got out of bed again, pulled on his T-shirt and shorts and went quietly down the attic stairs. He padded along the landing, down the stairs, and across the hall. Moonlight shone through the window above the front door. He turned the key in the lock, put the latch on so he could get back in, and ran softly over the road to the Wilderness.

The cool of the air washed over him.

Already he felt better.

The night was still. There was hardly any sound, now. The grass was damp under his bare feet. He stung his leg on a nettle but he didn't care. He slipped as easily and naturally as a wild creature, under the old pear tree, through the long grass, skirted the edge of the brambles, and sat on one of the logs in the place they'd had the campfire.

His breathing steadied. His heart stopped racing. His fists uncurled.

He knew the deer would come.

It had to.

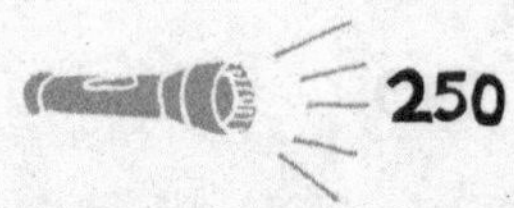

He willed it with his whole being.

*

His eyes strained into the dark. The moonlight barely penetrated the dense canopy of leaves, down here. He shivered. He waited and waited, and still nothing came. No deer, not a bat or a shrew or a scurrying mouse. Nothing at all.

He'd almost given up.

Something in his pocket bumped his leg. Noah fished out Mum's little digital camera. He'd borrowed it from her earlier in the week, just in case. And he'd forgotten it was still there.

He turned it on. There was a special setting for night-time.

A sudden movement over by the pond caught his eye.

A shadow.

The shadow took on form, and substance.

Noah watched, holding his breath, as the young deer dipped its head and lapped at the pond.

Very, very slowly, he held out the camera. Carefully, trying not to shake, he pressed the button.

Even that tiny sound was enough. In a flash, the deer had raced away.

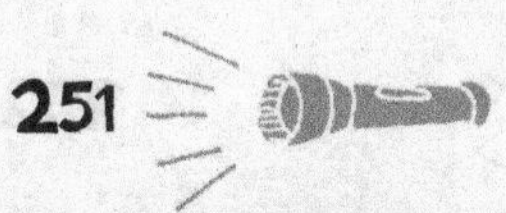

Noah crept back to the house. He waited till he was back in the attic, before he let himself check the camera image.

Shadowy, out of focus, but there: one young deer, eyes shining in the flash.

Evidence beyond all doubt.

Tuesday 5th August

Chapter 31

August 5th. Ten-thirty in the morning. Toby and Holly's dad slammed the boot of the car shut. 'Just about fitted everything in,' he said.

'Well done,' Toby and Holly's mum said. 'Thanks, Rob. I'll see you all at the meeting.'

'I wish we could all go together in one car,' Holly said.

'No room, I'm afraid.'

Toby sat in the front passenger seat; Noah squashed up with Holly and Nat in the back.

Noah felt sicker than ever.

'Meet us in the car park, near the library,' Holly yelled through the open car window, as Anil and Asha's mum

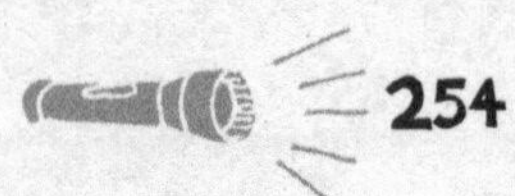

drove slowly past them up the hill.

Anil, Asha, and Zeke waved from the back seat. Phoebe did the thumbs up sign. Her hair looked funny. She'd done it differently, in a pulled-back-tight ponytail.

The engine started.

Noah sat on his hands to keep them from shaking. Deep in his pocket nestled the photo he had hastily printed off this morning, in secret. Like a talisman, reminding him why this mattered, and keeping him safe.

*

'Hurry up, Dad!' Toby kept checking his watch. 'The meeting starts at eleven.'

'Didn't expect town to be so busy.' Toby's dad drummed his fingers on the dashboard. 'If the worst comes to the worst I'll drop you off at the Town Hall while I go and find a parking space.'

'What! They might not let us in!' Holly squawked.

'Toby knows where the room is, don't you? I'll be as quick as I can.'

The traffic lights changed. Slowly, they edged forward. The traffic slowed, then stopped completely.

'We're not going to make it in time. I'll have to drop you

all here. I'll catch you up soon as.'

They piled out of the car. Each took a banner. Holly tucked the rolled-up map under her arm.

Toby and Holly's dad leaned over. 'You've got five minutes. *Run*. Good luck!'

The pavements were crowded with shoppers.

Noah and the others ran and shoved their way along.

People tutted. 'Such bad manners!' 'Youth of today . . . no patience.' 'What's the rush?'

'Please, let us through! It's an emergency!' Holly puffed, elbowing a large man in the middle of the pavement out of her way.

A girl holding her mum's hand read the words on the banners out loud. 'Save our Wilderness.'

'Well done, dears,' an old lady said. 'Good for you.'

Nearly there. Noah could see the impressive stone building of the Town Hall ahead now. At the top was a stone carving of old-fashioned weighing scales. It was supposed to represent Justice.

Anil, Asha, Phoebe, and a large squirrel rushed towards them. The squirrel was Zeke. 'At last! We were worried! We've only got one minute and fifty seconds. Come on!'

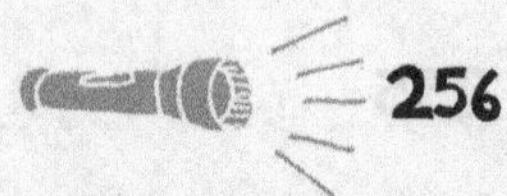

They raced up the steps and pushed through the big wooden swing doors into the large foyer. Three people in smart uniforms sitting behind a large wooden counter stared. The stares changed to frowns. The man in the middle stood up. A buzzer sounded.

A uniformed security guard clipped across the marble floor. 'Whoa! What's going on here?'

'Planning Application Meeting. Room twenty-three, 11 a.m. We know the way.' Toby tried to push past her.

'Not so fast, young man. This is not a playground. We can't have children on their own in council meetings.' She nodded at Zeke. 'No squirrels, either.'

Anil spoke up. 'That's age discrimination. We have rights too. Legal ones.'

Asha joined in. 'Yes. And in a democracy, you have to listen to everyone's views. Freedom of speech is enshrined in European law.'

The security guard smiled. She seemed to find them amusing. 'But there are rules. And one of the rules is, children at council meetings must be accompanied by an adult.'

'That's me!' Toby and Holly's dad came flying through

the swing doors, hair sticking up, his Pet Shop Boys T-shirt flapping. 'I'm the responsible adult!' he panted.

The guard looked him up and down. 'And these are all *your* children?'

'Yes. Absolutely. All seven.'

'Eight,' Phoebe said.

'Quick, Dad. The meeting's about to start.' Holly tugged her dad's sleeve. 'Room twenty-three. Upstairs.'

'So, excuse us, madam,' Toby and Holly's dad said, 'we have some important business to attend to.'

The security lady shrugged. 'Very well. But there's to be *no heckling* in the meeting. No mucking about. You must keep your *large* family under control at all times.'

'Of course.'

They trooped past her and legged it up the grand staircase. Disapproving rich old men stared down at them from the gold-framed oil paintings on the pale grey walls as they scuttled past. Phoebe stuck her tongue out at them.

The door to room twenty-three was closing. Zeke sprinted ahead to keep the door open for the rest of them.

Noah came in last. He sat down at the end of the row of chairs at the back, next to Holly. The room was small, but

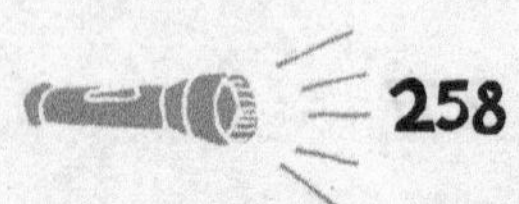

surprisingly full of people. They all seemed to be looking this way. For a while he couldn't see anything properly. His heart drummed in his chest. He kept having to swallow.

Once he'd calmed down a bit, he could take more in. Lots of the neighbours from the street were in the audience. And there were his own mum and dad, smiling and waving just behind Dr Gupta and Toby and Holly's mum, in the second row. Nat waved back.

A woman at the front cleared her throat. She was the person in charge. Six other people sat either side of her at a large polished table, each with a stack of papers before them.

'Welcome to this Planning Committee meeting of 5 August,' she began. 'And as it's unusual to have quite so many people in attendance at a council meeting, bear with me while I outline our official procedures.'

Her voice droned on. It was like school assembly, but worse, because there was no singing or standing up. They had lots of cases to hear, the lady said, and they would take them in a certain order. If anyone needed to leave the room at any point they should not come back in until a suitable break. No one must speak unless invited to by the chair.

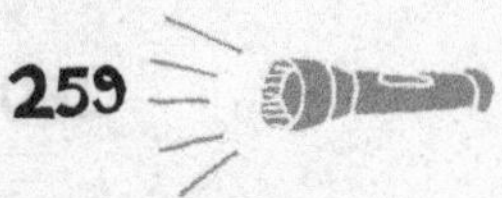

The *chair?*

It turned out that meant her, the lady.

It was hot in the room. The council lady poured glasses of water for her team of officials, but there were no refreshments for anyone else. Luckily Holly and Toby's dad had brought mini cartons of juice.

Holly nudged Noah. 'They've put us last, on purpose. Bet they think we'll give up and go away.'

Zeke unzipped his furry squirrel costume. He'd gone a peculiar shade of red.

Nat fidgeted and squirmed in her seat the other side of Holly.

The voices went on and on and on.

Noah stared at a wasp buzzing along the high-up window, trying to get out. At one point, someone official took a long pole with a hook on the end and opened the window. Noah imagined using it to pick pears off a tall tree . . . or it might make a good flagpole . . . or to scull a boat.

He daydreamed through the long, tedious meeting.

Words . . .

. . . and words . . .

. . . and more words.

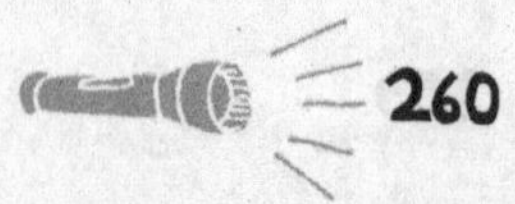

Every so often he tried to pay attention. A man with a beard talked about planning policy guidance for bringing vacant and underused land and buildings back into beneficial use . . . and another man asked him to define the word beneficial.

Phoebe, Nat, and Holly passed notes between them. Zeke slumped into a sleeping position and closed his eyes. Toby helped his dad solve a sudoku puzzle in the local paper. Anil tried to open his juice carton and squirted himself in the face. Phoebe giggled. Of all of them, only Asha looked keen and interested in the meeting, as if she found every little detail fascinating.

It all took such a long time Noah forgot to be quite so nervous any more. His stomach rumbled. It must be lunchtime by now.

Holly nudged him again.

'So, we come to Planning Application number thirteen, for the potential development of houses on a patch of derelict land opposite Pear Tree Buildings, by Mr Malcolm Treasure.'

'This is us,' Holly whispered to Noah. 'We're on.'

Chapter 32

A man near the front of the room stood up. 'I'm Mr Treasure,' he said. 'A few words, if I may.'

Noah stared. There he was at last: their arch-enemy. In real life he was just a middle-aged man in a suit, with pale brown, thinning hair and a pointy face—a bit like a weasel, Noah thought, remembering Mr Moss.

'Sit down, please, Mr Treasure,' the council lady said. 'We have the papers here for your application. We don't hear from you directly at this point of the meeting.'

But Mr Treasure would not sit down. 'I must emphasize the point that people in this city need homes, and this is a prime location that has become derelict wasteland and an

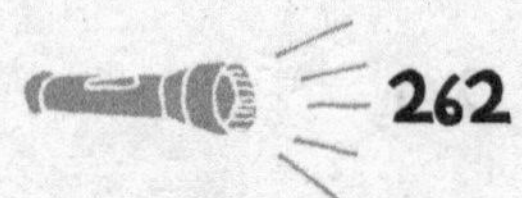

eyesore to local residents.'

The council lady was cross. 'I can have you thrown out,' she said, 'if you don't listen to the rules. Now sit down and be quiet.'

Toby and Zeke went '*Whoop!*'—but under their breath, so as not to get into trouble.

Mr Treasure sat down, muttering.

There was much shuffling of papers up the front, and the council lady read out the application for removal of overgrown trees and building of five detached houses on the patch of derelict land opposite Pear Tree Buildings.

'*Five houses?*' someone at the front said. 'Ridiculous! *That's* the eyesore, not the lovely trees.'

The lady passed a map and some photographs around the table at the front.

'We'll move straight to the objections,' the council lady said, looking at her watch. 'Due to the time pressures we can only hear objections that have been formally registered in writing in advance, as per council planning meeting rules sub-clause five, section three, paragraph one.'

Toby looked at Holly, and then at Noah. '*Whaaaat?*'

'Shush!' A grumpy man glared at them.

'It's OK, I registered us,' Asha whispered. 'It's all fine.'

'So,' the lady glanced at her papers. 'We will hear the objection registered by Mr and Ms A. Gupta, please.'

Asha and Anil stood up.

A ripple of amusement went through the room. They'd been expecting two grown-ups.

Asha led the way to the front.

'Come on, everybody!' Anil pulled Holly, Nat, and Toby after him.

Zeke zipped up his squirrel suit. He handed out photos to the people in the audience as he followed after Toby.

Phoebe tightened her ponytail, picked up a banner in each hand and clip-clopped to the front too. She, Holly, and Natalie held the banners high.

SAVE OUR LAND!

GREEN SPACES FOR CITY KIDS!

SAVE OUR WILDERNESS.

Noah crouched lower in his seat, sick to the stomach. He couldn't stand up there. He just couldn't. They'd be fine without him.

Anil placed his mum's laptop on the table and clicked onto the first slide: a beautiful photo of a tortoiseshell butterfly projected onto the wall behind the committee. Most people smiled and relaxed as Anil clicked through more images. The grumpy man at the back growled, 'Get on with it,' but everyone else shushed him.

Natalie and Holly unrolled the map and held it up.

People in the front rows gasped.

'Oh my,' a lady said. 'Isn't that just bea-ut-if-ul!'

Toby held up his clipboard and began. 'This council itself has a policy to provide "green lungs" in the city, to promote health and well-being, and provide open space in accessible locations.' He looked very pleased with all the long words he'd used. He sounded very official.

'You call this "derelict land",' Toby continued, 'but if you look more closely you will see that there is nothing derelict about it. It is, in fact, a small patch of wild paradise in the middle of the city, a haven for wildlife, such as frogs and toads, butterflies and beetles, damsel and dragonflies and many species of nesting birds.'

Mr Treasure sighed deeply and noisily. 'Give me strength!' he muttered.

Everyone else in the room was quiet, listening.

Holly took over from Toby. 'And this little patch of land is more than a home for wildlife. It is a very special place where we children can run about, climb trees, play tag and explore stuff and use our imaginations and be happy outdoors, which grown-ups like the government and teachers and the media keep saying is really important for being healthy. We don't have back gardens, so this place is extra special to us. And I bet lots of you played out the whole time when you were young, back in the olden days. So why shouldn't we?'

Someone laughed. A woman clapped and others joined in.

Mr Treasure tried to interrupt. 'This city has parks and playgrounds and play schemes galore—'

'Excuse me, but shut up and listen,' Phoebe said. 'It's our turn, not yours!'

Lots of people cheered from the front row. Phoebe did an elaborate stage bow, and they clapped her some more.

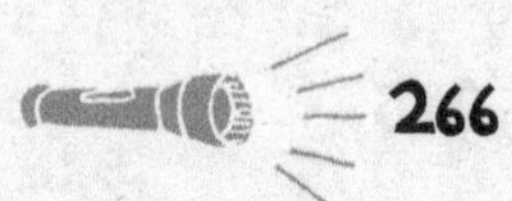

'And in any case, that's totally different,' Anil said. 'We're talking about free play, and having adventures, and taking risks. Our own wild places close to our homes where we don't need adults to take us in the car.' He clicked onto the next photos, of the dens, and the pond, and the close-up of the damselflies.

'And now please listen to the oldest resident in the street.'

Mr Moss's face filled the screen, larger than life, crinkly and weather-beaten.

People leaned forward to listen as he spoke about his childhood and life in the street, and his garden and the birds and nests, and precious moments like watching the sunset behind the ash trees and hearing the dawn chorus in spring. He was an old man: he had few pleasures. This meant the world to him . . .

'Emotional blackmail!' Mr Treasure muttered loudly.

'And you should be ashamed of yourselves,' Mr Moss said quietly but determinedly to camera. 'Leaving it to the children to defend this precious place. So, I say a big thank you to the children, who know what matters and have the guts to speak up for it against the forces of money and greed.'

Anil clicked the next slide.

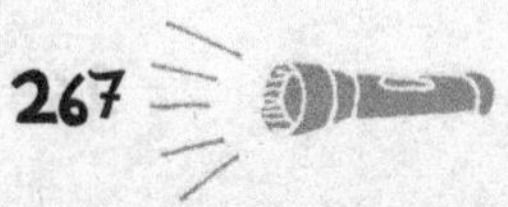

The photograph of Noah and Crow filled the screen.

The hairs on the back of Noah's neck prickled. It was weird, seeing himself up there, and everyone looking. Like being in a film.

Noah saw his parents glance at each other and clasp hands. His mum's eyes were all watery.

Asha spoke up. 'Not only all this, but there is a legal precedent going back to the 1880s for any owner of the land to allow residents in Pear Tree Buildings to buy or rent the strip opposite their houses, as shown in this map of 1884.'

Anil clicked on the map, scanned onto the computer.

Asha took a deep breath 'To summarize: the people actually living in Pear Tree Buildings have a first right to the land. The sale and development of the land cannot proceed.'

Had they said enough? Would the Council Planning Committee be convinced? Everything depended on this.

Mr Treasure scraped his chair noisily across the wooden floor as he stood up. 'Ha!' he said triumphantly. 'Got you! *I* own the houses at the top of the street, numbers thirty-three to thirty-one, and twenty-eight and twenty-nine. So it's *my* land and I am entitled to do what I like, and what I like is

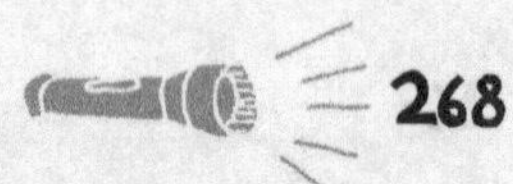

to improve and develop it and build a few very nice houses. So there.'

There was a horrible, long silence. The planning committee people flipped through the papers in front of them.

Noah watched Holly. She was waving at him, mouthing something . . .

'Noah?' she called out. '*Please?* For the sake of the Wilderness.'

Noah swallowed hard.

Something about the way Holly looked at him—her dark eyes, her direct gaze—made him think of the wild deer, in the early morning light.

He took a deep breath. It was now or never. He *had* to speak out, however scared he was. He knew that so suddenly and clearly, that he stood up and walked to the front of the room, barely noticing how much he was shaking.

'The boy with the bird!' someone said.

Holly shuffled closer to him. He felt her presence, willing him courage.

He swallowed hard, and began.

Chapter 33

'My name is Noah,' he began. His voice came out too soft at first.

A hush fell over the room.

'I live in Pear Tree Buildings, like Toby and Holly and Asha and Anil and Zeke and Natalie and Phoebe. And *unlike* Mr Treasure, who does not. So to him this is just a piece of land he can make money out of.

'But for us it is a special place. A rare wild place in the middle of the city where we can play and have fun, but also home to lots of creatures that Mr Treasure has probably never noticed. And those insects and plants and animals and birds'—at this point, Anil cleverly clicked back to the

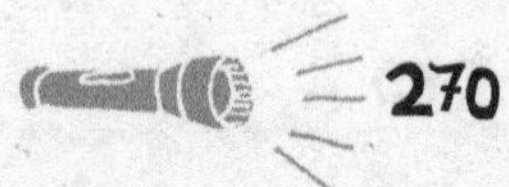

picture of Noah and Crow—'don't have a voice. So I am speaking for them.'

His face was hot, but he didn't care any longer. This might be the moment that changed everything. He spoke from his heart. The words just came, without him having to think at all. His voice got louder.

'The most important thing is, that whoever owns the land, it stays wild. Exactly as it is. Not neat and tidied up and prettified, like a garden or a park or a playground. It needs to be a wild place, with fallen trees and brambles and nettles for the butterflies and insects to feed on and birds to nest in.

'Mr Treasure says he can do what he likes with his bit of the land, but that's not true. Everything is connected. Like in nature. Anything he does will affect everyone else's bit of the Wilderness. If you build houses at the top, and diggers and builders come on the land and more people and traffic in the street, then the wild creatures will disappear. We will lose everything that is precious.'

Noah had never said so much in one go, and certainly never in front of so many people. But his voice came clear and strong, and his heartbeat steadied, as he talked about

the things that he loved. Now, he could see people smiling, and nodding, encouraging him.

'It's the best thing ever to get up early and dive deep into the long grass of the Wilderness. Really early, the birds sing their heads off and it's like the world's just waking up, as if before all the city and human noise gets loud and smothers it, the wild world has its own special time.

'And this summer, I found a baby crow and made friends with him, and he's not a pet; he's still wild, but he trusts me. And that's amazing.'

Noah took a deep breath. 'Sometimes I lie in the long grass on a hot day and watch the grasshoppers and the ants and the beetles getting on with their lives and the sun's warm on my back and I can forget everything else, like worries and school and stuff. And we can camp out all night in the summer, and cook on a little fire and watch the stars. And there's hardly anywhere in the city you can do that when you're a child and it's really important, and if people don't love nature then everything starts to go wrong. And lots of grown-ups know that deep down, but they forget.'

Noah's legs were shaking. He looked directly at the

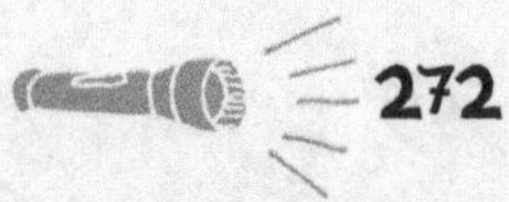

audience. 'The Wilderness is the one place where I can really be me.'

'And sometimes . . .' he summoned up his last reserves of courage, 'there's even a young deer who somehow finds his way into the city, to graze on our Wilderness grass in the early morning. It's totally magical.' He fumbled in his pocket, drew out the paper print-out of the photo, smoothed the creases and held it up with trembling hands.

'Ohhhhhh.' A sort of collective sigh went round the room, like a breath of wind, as people saw the deer.

'Oh wow,' Holly whispered, standing close behind him. 'That was wonderful, Noah.'

'Bravo!' someone called from the second row.

'Well said, lad.'

Noah's mum and dad clapped and stamped their feet. Others joined in. A man called out, 'Three cheers for the kids! Bring on the revolution!'

'*Stop!*' the council lady shouted. 'Everybody, stop talking immediately! This meeting is totally out of order. Children taking over, and people shouting out, and no one following the rules: it's a disgrace!'

There was a brief, heated conversation between her and

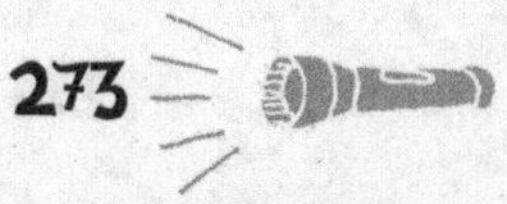

the committee people at the table. They shook their heads. The council lady stood up again.

'The committee cannot approve this planning application.'

'*Yay!*' Toby punched the air.

Holly, Asha, Phoebe, and Nat did a little dance of joy on the spot.

'Well done!' 'Brilliant!' People called out, and cheered and stamped their feet.

The children cheered loudest of all.

'The objection is upheld. No building can go ahead on this small and evidently important piece of wild land. Our wildlife officer will visit the site in question to make further recommendations for its protection. This meeting is now ended.' The council lady sank back in her seat.

Mr Treasure stormed out of the room and slammed the door.

People crowded round the children and shook their hands. They oohed and ahhed over the map. They patted Anil and Asha on the back and told them how very professional they were. They admired Zeke's costume and stroked the fur.

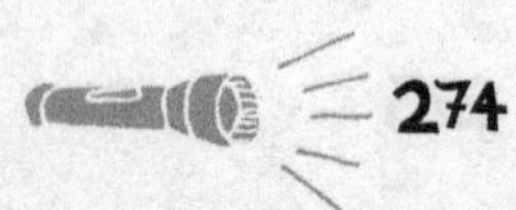

Everyone said Noah was a total star.

Toby and Holly's dad hurried over. He pushed through the scrum. 'Quick, outside, kids,' he said. He looked very pleased with himself. 'The press are waiting for you.'

Chapter 34

While the children were presenting their case at the front of the room, Toby and Holly's dad had texted the local paper about the children's campaign, and a reporter and photographer were waiting for them in the foyer downstairs.

He cleared the way for them. 'Make way, excuse us, mind your backs,' he shouted, as if they were celebrities. It was funny, seeing the effect this had. The crowd parted to let them through. Other people cottoned on to the fact that something big was happening, and whipped out their mobile phones to snap pictures as Noah and the others ran down the elegant stone stairs.

The photographer arranged them with their banners and map in front of a large display of silk lilies and plastic ferns in the foyer. 'Amazing!' she said. 'Now, all turn this way; look very sad and disappointed.'

'Why?' Holly said. 'We're actually extremely pleased and excited. We won our case!'

'Oh, a group of sweet little children looking sad will tug at the heartstrings better,' the photographer said. 'Our *Chronicle* readers love that.'

'YUCK!—' Holly started, but she saw her dad's face and stopped herself. He had arranged all this. It was his way of trying to help.

Phoebe loved the fuss. So did Zeke: in his squirrel costume, he was particularly photogenic.

Mum hugged Noah and kissed the top of his head before he had time to duck. 'So proud of you, wild boy!'

Natalie grabbed her hand and dragged her away to the toilets. 'Quick, Mum! I've been dying to go all morning!'

Noah just wanted to go home. This was his worst nightmare. He wriggled his way into the back of the group so he was mostly hidden behind Toby.

Toby and Holly's dad had told their story to the reporter

already.

'Your names?' the reporter asked the children, pen poised.

'You shouldn't use their actual names,' Toby's dad said. 'Just say, a *bunch of intrepid young people* bravely defended a unique patch of wild land against the greedy, selfish grasp of a money-grabbing capitalist developer. That should do the trick.'

The reporter wrote that down. 'How do you spell *intrepid*?'

Toby told him.

'Will we be on the telly news?' Zeke asked.

'No, the local paper,' the reporter said. 'Next Thursday week. We're fortnightly, these days.'

Zeke looked a bit disappointed.

But Noah was relieved. He'd had enough publicity for one day.

'Now, celebration time. The finest organic farm-made ice creams for all,' Toby and Holly's dad said. 'I'm paying. Have whatever you want. Mango and blackcurrant's pretty good. We'll go to the Puppet Theatre Café down by the river.'

They got home mid-afternoon. Mr Moss was standing at

his gate. He waved as they tumbled out of the car. Holly and Noah went to speak to him.

'How'd it go?'

'We won. They turned down the planning application,' Holly said.

Mr Moss nodded. 'Quite right too.'

'And now we know about owning our strip of the Wilderness, Noah's mum and dad might buy theirs, and the Guptas, and maybe some of the other neighbours, too. There were lots of them at the meeting. So the Wilderness will be safe forever.' Holly hopped up and down off the kerb with happiness.

'That's good, lass,' Mr Moss said. He handed Noah a small paper bag.

'What is it?'

'Mealworms, dried,' Mr Moss said. 'A treat for Crow.'

'Thanks,' Noah said.

'You'll be glad when all the fuss and bother's died down,' Mr Moss said.

Noah nodded. Mr Moss was dead right about that.

'I've seen how good you all are at making things,' Mr Moss said. 'Think you might find some old rubbish to put

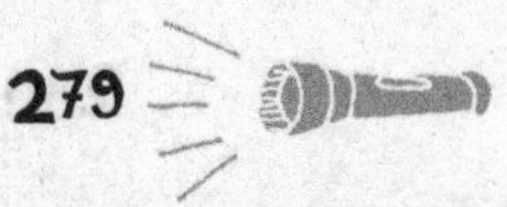

together a sort of a seat, for me? Then I can sit down, rest me old pegs, get a bit of fresh air meself out here. Watch the birds and that.'

'Oh yes,' Holly said. 'We'd love to make you a bench, wouldn't we, Noah?'

'Yes,' Noah said.

Phoebe skipped down the street to join them. 'Did you hear how brilliant we were?'

Mr Moss smiled. 'I did. I knew you would be.'

'Everyone *loved* your speech,' Phoebe said. You're quite the celebrity now.'

Mr Moss did a mock bow.

'We'd have bought you a thank-you ice cream,' Phoebe said, 'only it would have melted.'

'Another time,' Mr Moss said. 'And make it a strawberry one, please.'

'Of course! With extra strawberry bits and a chocolate flake.'

'And we're going to have a celebration bonfire tonight and invite the whole street,' Holly said. 'You'll come, won't you? We'll cook sausages and marshmallows and my dad's going to bring fizzy wine and beer for the grown-ups.'

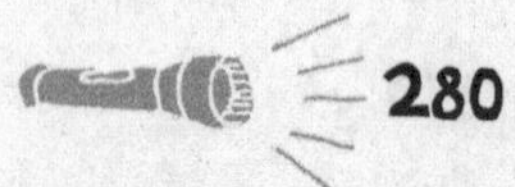

'Lovely stuff,' Mr Moss said. 'I'll come and raise a glass to the Wilderness.'

Crow flew down onto the greenhouse roof. He'd spotted Noah. He croaked three times.

Noah ran across the road. He rattled the paper bag and poured a small heap of dried mealworms onto a flat stone for Crow.

Crow gobbled them up and asked for more.

'You'll get lazy,' Noah said. 'You'll stop finding food for yourself.'

It was such a relief to be outside, free again. He carried on downhill to the dump, to see if there were any old bits of wood for a bench, and some bricks perhaps, to rest it on. He liked the idea of a seat for Mr Moss. Maybe he was a bit lonely. If he sat outside, more people would talk to him, like they did Noah's Nana.

People were a mystery, Noah thought. People kept on chucking their rubbish over the fence, as if it was perfectly all right to do that. Today the new stuff was a load of stinking grass clippings, some empty beer cans and a pile of rubble and some rotten wood. He rummaged through, but there weren't any big enough bits for a bench. He skirted along the fence.

Crow hopped along the top, keeping pace with him.

Asha was making clay beads near her den. She dug around in the boggy patch, found patches of clay, poured water on it to soften it and make it go squidgy, then scooped it up, moulding it with her fingers into the shapes she wanted. She left the beads to dry in the sun. Later she would paint them with bright enamel paint. She was so absorbed in what she was doing, she hardly noticed Noah. Anil lay on his stomach reading a book. He looked up briefly, waved, and carried on reading.

Noah heard Holly, Natalie, and Phoebe's voices; the three of them were sitting in the pirate ship den, discussing where to go next and who was going to be captain (Holly, obviously, but Phoebe wanted a go) and what they'd do when they got there . . .

Noah went back via the bramble den. He picked a small handful of ripe blackberries and ate them. The taste was like the taste of all the other summers.

He zigzagged through the grass uphill, towards the tall ash trees.

The crow family was squabbling as usual. The babies from the second brood were almost ready to fledge.

Noah watched as Crow flew up to the old nest and was scolded away by the parent birds.

'You'll have to make a nest of your own, Crow!' Noah told him.

Where did Crow sleep at night? He'd not thought about it before. And what did happen, when birds left the nest and grew up? Did they simply perch somewhere safe and tuck their head under their wing? He'd seen ducks do that, on the edge of the old canal that curved away from the city. Starlings roosted together under bridges. Pigeons, too, flocked together. But crows were solitary birds.

So much he didn't know.

So many exciting things to find out.

Noah climbed up his tree. He'd done it so often his hands and feet knew exactly where to go.

He settled on his wooden platform with his back against the smooth grey trunk. The leaves above him made delicious green shade. They rustled in the breeze. That was a summery sound. In the spring, when the leaves were fresh and new, they'd make a different one.

It was only August, but already, the ash seeds were ripening ready for autumn.

Noah surveyed the scene from his high perch.

The world seemed bigger than ever from up here.

There was Zeke, with his mum and his big sister Dani, getting into her car, going off to buy the sausages for the party.

Toby's dad stopped for a chat with Mr Moss and then walked down the hill to number seven. He unloaded a big cardboard box of wine from the car.

The pirate ship had the sail up, and now a small blue flag fluttered at the top of the mast too, alongside the skull and crossbones. They were sailing to far-off islands. Beyond the limits of the known world, further than the edge of the map.

What now? Noah thought.

Nothing, that's what.

He'd sit up here, and do absolutely nothing.

And later, they'd make the fire, and have a party with all the neighbours. They'd never done that before. It would be strange, sharing their special place with all the grown-ups. But if that's what saving the Wilderness meant, that's what they'd do.

Deep down, Noah had a sense that soon enough the adults would be busy again with other stuff, and he and

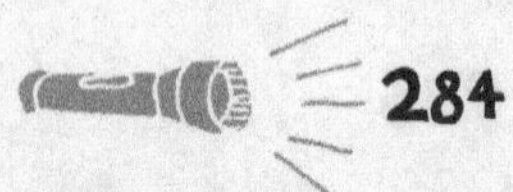

his friends would have their Wilderness back again all to themselves. Them, and the birds and grasshoppers, the butterflies and bats, the moths and the dragonflies and spiders and snails and bees and beetles.

Maybe, in time, there would even be newts.

Chapter 35

All eight of them lay on their backs in a semi-circle around the embers of the fire, looking out for shooting stars. Noah had that happy feeling of being in his favourite place, with his friends, a full stomach, and—finally—nothing to worry about.

Everyone had loved the party.

'We'll do it again,' Mum said as she cleared up the last paper plates and cups. 'It's good to bring the neighbours together round a bonfire.'

Noah had showed people the pond. Anil and Asha did a tour of the dens. Mr Moss couldn't manage to walk over the bumpy ground, but he sat on the chair Phoebe had carried down specially, ate sausages, and went all giggly after his glass of fizzy wine. Later, the grown-ups had gone home, to carry on the party inside Asha and Anil's house.

'It's not dark enough to see shooting stars,' Zeke said.

'Keep looking. It's getting darker all the time. Cup your hands round your face so you shut out the streetlights,' Holly said.

'There'll be loads, soon,' Noah said. 'Like, sixty or a hundred in just one hour.'

'And you can make a wish on each one you see,' Holly said.

'There's one!' Asha pointed.

'No, that's a satellite!' Anil said. 'You can tell, the way it sort of clicks round on a regular route. A star would whoosh.'

'I wish . . .' Phoebe started.

Nat stopped her. 'You mustn't *say* what you wish out loud. It won't come true if you do.'

'And you haven't seen a shooting star, yet,' Toby said.

'This time next week, Toby and me will be looking at stars in France,' Holly said.

'And we might be on a beach somewhere,' Nat said, 'with our Nana.'

'It's not fair. We never go anywhere,' Phoebe said.

'Nor do we,' Zeke said. 'So you'll be stuck with me all the rest of the holidays.'

'And us!' Asha and Anil said quickly together. 'We'll be here too.'

'Shooting star! There! Quick!'

'And another!'

'Wish, everyone!'

Noah shut his eyes to wish harder. He wished with all his heart, and he knew that the others, close beside him, were wishing too. And although no one actually said anything out loud, he had a feeling they all wished for the same thing. Wilderness wishes, to keep it safe forever.

*

One by one, they staggered home to bed.

It was just Toby and Noah left now.

'Good you got that photo of the deer,' Toby said. 'Everyone was well impressed.'

Noah didn't say anything.

'That wildlife officer's going to come and see what else we've got here.'

Noah didn't answer.

'That's good, isn't it?' Toby said.

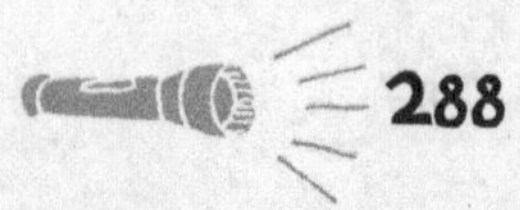

‘I guess.’ It was hard, sharing his Wilderness with other people. But it would get easier with practice.

‘Toby?’ Holly called from the street. ‘Dad’s leaving soon.’

Toby scrambled up. ‘Got to go. See you tomorrow.’

*

Noah climbed up the ash tree to sit in his lookout.

Something moved, just above his head.

Noah looked up. It was too dark to see much, but the dark something hopped closer.

‘Hello, Crow.’ Noah settled back against the tree trunk, and Crow hopped down to settle next to him.

‘We did it, Crow,’ Noah said.

The bird put his head on one side, listening.

Noah fished in his pocket. Breadcrumbs, from the sausage baps. He held them out, and Crow pecked from his hand, quite gently considering how sharp his beak was.

Noah thought again about the meeting. He could hardly believe he’d done that, now. Speaking out in front of all those people! And the clapping, afterwards!

‘People loved seeing the photo of you and me together,’ Noah told Crow. ‘We might be in the newspaper, too.’

‘Craaw,’ said Crow, as if he understood.

'But this is better than all of that. Just you and me, in the tree, in our wild Wilderness.'

Noah yawned. It had been such a long, busy day. Even so, he'd stay here with Crow a little longer.

He'd wait to see the very last shooting star.

And maybe a bit longer than that, if he could keep his eyes open.

Because this was the perfect kind of night for a shy young deer to come stepping softly through the long grass,

ears alert,

nose twitching,

taking his place in the Wilderness.

Noah's notes on Bees

There are about 250 different types of bees in the UK:

24 species of bumblebees

225 species of solitary bees*

ONE kind of honey bee.

* Solitary bees don't live in colonies, produce honey or have a queen. They are FANTASTIC pollinators (better than honey bees) so are a GOOD THING! They don't swarm, or get angry. Each female solitary bee makes her own nest.

There are two main kinds you can see:

- Mining bees, which nest in underground burrows, and
- Cavity bees, which need dry hollow tubes to nest in (you can make a DIY bee house,

to help them! See the GROW WILD website www.growwilduk.com)

Bees feed on the nectar and pollen made in flowers.

Bees are in TROUBLE because there are fewer WILDFLOWERS these days, and that means LESS FOOD for bees.

WHAT CAN WE DO?

GROW BEE-FRIENDLY flowers in our gardens and on grass verges, and in parks, and everywhere! Try crocus, snowdrop, winter aconite, ivy, fruit trees (e.g. pears, cherry, apple), primroses, foxgloves, marigolds, lavender, cornflowers, geraniums, forget-me-nots, poppies, dog rose, blackberries, evening primrose, ox-eye daisies, nasturtiums, herbs like marjoram & thyme, and loads more.

If you are going to make a campfire then make sure you have a grown-up on hand to help out.

Always ask the landowner's permission before starting a campfire. Some landowners such as the Woodland Trust do not permit fires in their woods. Visit woodlandtrust.org.uk to find helpful information on woodland areas near you.

1. Choosing the right space

Choosing the right space to start your campfire is important. It needs to be a clearing at least three metres from any trees or shrubs that could catch alight.

2. Preparing the area

Clear a space about two metres wide for the fire, removing any grass, leaves and twigs. Then build a circle of stones around 1 metre across to contain your fire. Remember to keep water on hand in case you need to put the fire out.

Woodland Trust Nature detectives

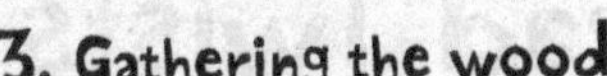

3. Gathering the wood

- **Tinder**—small dry twigs, leaves or grass.
- **Kindling**—thin dry sticks smaller than 2cm thick.
- **Fuel**—larger pieces of dry wood.

4. Constructing your fire

Create a ball of tinder in your hands and place it in the middle of the stone fire circle. Then add the kindling, leaning it into a point over the tinder, like a tepee.

5. Lighting your fire

Use a match to light the tinder. Once the tinder has fully started to burn, slowly add some small pieces of kindling, keeping the sticks close together but allowing space for air. Gradually increase the size of the kindling you add to the fire. When you have a good fire going, slowly add the fuel one piece at a time in the same way as the kindling, creating a tepee shape.

Remember to fully extinguish the fire when you're done, use plenty of water to make sure that no part of it is still burning.

Campfire Bread Twists

These delicious campfire treats are fun, and really easy to make.

You will need:

500g Self-raising flour
3 Tbs of sugar
1 Tsp of salt
300–500ml of water
Optional: Jam or honey

If you are going to make bread twists then make sure you have a grown-up on hand to help out.

Always ask the landowner's permission before starting a campfire. Some landowners such as the Woodland Trust do not permit fires in their woods. Visit woodlandtrust.org.uk to find helpful information on woodland areas near you.

Start by mixing the sugar, salt and flour in a large bowl. Once the sugar and flour are combined, add about 200-300ml of water and mix. Keep adding small amounts of water—and knead the dough forming it into one big lump. Keep kneading until the dough becomes smooth and springy, then it's ready.

Leave the dough to one side while you prepare your cooking stick. Choose a sturdy-looking stick, around 2.5cm thick, and strip off the bark and leaves.

Now you're ready to get cooking. Grab a small handful of dough and roll it into a snake-like shape. This won't need to be very thick, as the dough will swell when cooking. Next, twist your dough onto the stick.

To cook your bread, hold the stick over the embers of a campfire. If you hold it directly into the flames it's likely to burn. Once it starts to turn golden brown it's cooked and ready to eat. Your campfire bread twist will taste great as is, or with jam or honey.

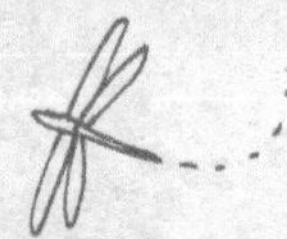

Frog Pond

Follow these simple steps to create a mini frog pond.

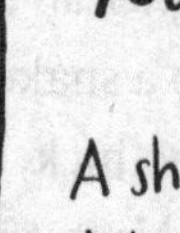

You will need:

A shovel
A large container
Old bricks or bits of wood
Some small pond plants

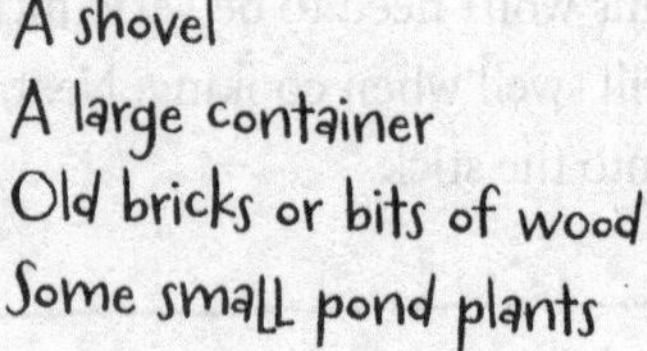

If you are going to make a frog pond then make sure you have a grown-up on hand to help out.

1. Choose your container. This could be a washing up bowl, bucket, or even an old sink. Keep in mind this is something which will have to be strong enough to withstand bad weather.

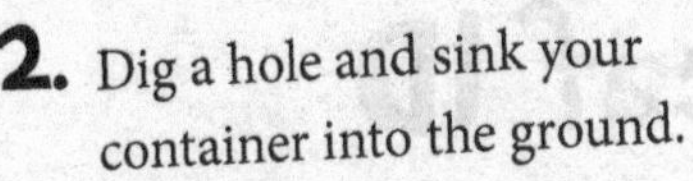

2. Dig a hole and sink your container into the ground.

3. Make sure that wildlife can get in and out, by using bricks or wood to create stepping stones in and out of the pond.

4. Use rainwater to fill your pond, as tap water is harmful to pond life.

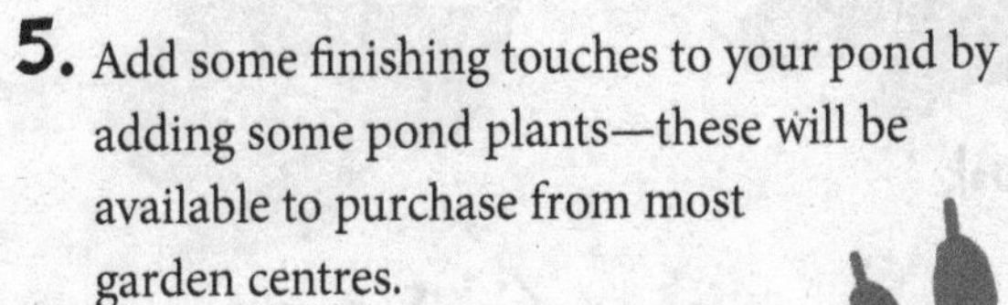

5. Add some finishing touches to your pond by adding some pond plants—these will be available to purchase from most garden centres.

Many ponds may not get froggy visitors, but birds may visit for drinking/bathing, mammals too, and of course all sorts of minibeasts!

Leaf ID

Be a super spotter!
How many trees can you identify?

Woodland Trust
Nature
detectives
Field Maple
Birch
Holly
Horse Chestnut
Rowan
Hawthorn
Hazel
Go online for lots more activities:
www.woodlandtrust.org.uk/naturedetectives

Den building!

Be a real Nature Detective and make your own woodland den.

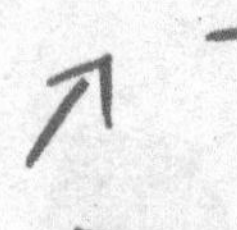

Please don't cut anything down or damage anything while building your den.

1. Find a good foundation

This will form the base of your framework, so keep your eyes peeled for a strong tree with suitable nooks, crannies and knobbly bits.

2. Build your framework

Find a couple of large branches and wedge them firmly together against the tree. If your chosen tree has a strong, low branch, even better! You can use this instead.

3. Build the walls

Collect more branches and rest them against your framework. Make sure you pack them closely together so that they're strong and secure.

4. Protect your den from the elements

Use smaller branches, twigs, leaves and moss to cover your den. Remember to push them into any gaps so that your den shelters you from wind and rain.

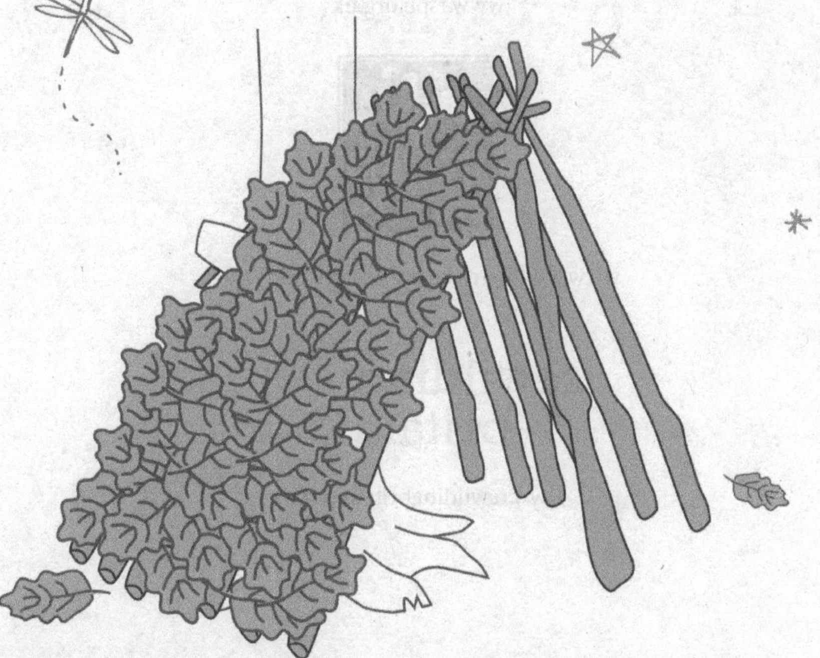

Other useful websites for further information:

woodlandtrust.org.uk

giving
nature
a home

www.rspb.org.uk

www.wildlifetrusts.org/EveryChildWild

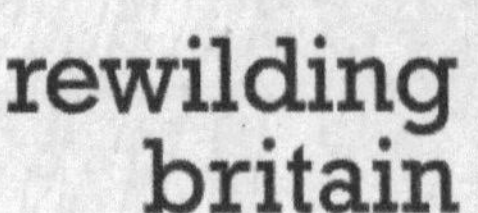

www.rewildingbritain.org.uk

Julia Green

Julia lives in Bath. Many wild birds and foxes, deer, squirrels and badgers come to visit her wild and unruly garden most days. She has two grown-up sons who are both passionate about wilderness (one loves the mountains, the other is sailing around the world on a small boat). She is the Course Director for the MA Writing for Young People at Bath Spa University, which has launched the careers of many children's authors, and has written more than sixteen books for children and young adults. Julia's favourite places are wild remote islands, beaches, cliffs and hill-tops. One day, maybe she'll live somewhere like that.

You can find out more about Julia on her website **www.julia-green.co.uk** and follow her author page on Facebook.

Acknowledgements

Thank you as ever to my wonderful colleagues and friends in the Writing for Young People team at Bath Spa University, especially Steve, Lucy, Janine and David; to Nicola Davies, best of wild companions; to my loving family, and especially to my sons and nephews, whose wild games were my inspiration. Thank you to Clare and Gillian and the team of wonderful, creative people at Oxford University Press.

Ready for more great stories? You might like these . . .

Dreaming the Bear

Gorilla Dawn

Shadow Cat

Charlie Merrick's Misfits in I'm a Nobody, Get Me Out of Here!